FOR RAGE

(A Morgan Cross FBI Suspense Thriller—Book Two)

BLAKE PIERCE

Blake Pierce

Blake Pierce is the USA Today bestselling author of the RILEY PAGE mystery series, which includes seventeen books. Blake Pierce is also the author of the MACKENZIE WHITE mystery series, comprising fourteen books; of the AVERY BLACK mystery series, comprising six books; of the KERI LOCKE mystery series, comprising five books; of the MAKING OF RILEY PAIGE mystery series, comprising six books; of the KATE WISE mystery series, comprising seven books; of the CHLOE FINE psychological suspense mystery, comprising six books; of the JESSIE HUNT psychological suspense thriller series, comprising twenty-eight books; of the AU PAIR psychological suspense thriller series, comprising three books; of the ZOE PRIME mystery series, comprising six books; of the ADELE SHARP mystery series, comprising sixteen books, of the EUROPEAN VOYAGE cozy mystery series, comprising six books; of the LAURA FROST FBI suspense thriller, comprising eleven books; of the ELLA DARK FBI suspense thriller, comprising fourteen books (and counting); of the A YEAR IN EUROPE cozy mystery series, comprising nine books, of the AVA GOLD mystery series, comprising six books; of the RACHEL GIFT mystery series, comprising ten books (and counting); of the VALERIE LAW mystery series, comprising nine books (and counting); of the PAIGE KING mystery series, comprising eight books (and counting); of the MAY MOORE mystery series, comprising eleven books; of the CORA SHIELDS mystery series, comprising eight books (and counting); of the NICKY LYONS mystery series, comprising eight books (and counting), of the CAMI LARK mystery series, comprising eight books (and counting), of the AMBER YOUNG mystery series, comprising five books (and counting), of the DAISY FORTUNE mystery series, comprising five books (and counting), of the FIONA RED mystery series, comprising eight books (and counting), of the FAITH BOLD mystery series, comprising eight books (and counting), of the JULIETTE HART mystery series, comprising five books (and counting), of the MORGAN CROSS mystery series, comprising five books (and counting), and of the new FINN WRIGHT mystery series, comprising five books (and counting).

An avid reader and lifelong fan of the mystery and thriller genres, Blake loves to hear from you, so please feel free to visit www.blakepierceauthor.com to learn more and stay in touch.

ISBN: 978-1-0943-8230-2

BOOKS BY BLAKE PIERCE

FINN WRIGHT MYSTERY SERIES
WHEN YOU'RE MINE (Book #1)
WHEN YOU'RE SAFE (Book #2)
WHEN YOU'RE CLOSE (Book #3)
WHEN YOU'RE SLEEPING (Book #4)
WHEN YOU'RE SANE (Book #5)

MORGAN CROSS MYSTERY SERIES
FOR YOU (Book #1)
FOR RAGE (Book #2)
FOR LUST (Book #3)
FOR WRATH (Book #4)
FOREVER (Book #5)

JULIETTE HART MYSTERY SERIES
NOTHING TO FEAR (Book #1)
NOTHING THERE (Book #2)
NOTHING WATCHING (Book #3)
NOTHING HIDING (Book #4)
NOTHING LEFT (Book #5)

FAITH BOLD MYSTERY SERIES
SO LONG (Book #1)
SO COLD (Book #2)
SO SCARED (Book #3)
SO NORMAL (Book #4)
SO FAR GONE (Book #5)
SO LOST (Book #6)
SO ALONE (Book #7)
SO FORGOTTEN (Book #8)

FIONA RED MYSTERY SERIES
LET HER GO (Book #1)
LET HER BE (Book #2)
LET HER HOPE (Book #3)
LET HER WISH (Book #4)
LET HER LIVE (Book #5)
LET HER RUN (Book #6)
LET HER HIDE (Book #7)
LET HER BELIEVE (Book #8)

DAISY FORTUNE MYSTERY SERIES
NEED YOU (Book #1)
CLAIM YOU (Book #2)
CRAVE YOU (Book #3)
CHOOSE YOU (Book #4)
CHASE YOU (Book #5)

AMBER YOUNG MYSTERY SERIES
ABSENT PITY (Book #1)
ABSENT REMORSE (Book #2)
ABSENT FEELING (Book #3)
ABSENT MERCY (Book #4)
ABSENT REASON (Book #5)

CAMI LARK MYSTERY SERIES
JUST ME (Book #1)
JUST OUTSIDE (Book #2)
JUST RIGHT (Book #3)
JUST FORGET (Book #4)
JUST ONCE (Book #5)
JUST HIDE (Book #6)
JUST NOW (Book #7)
JUST HOPE (Book #8)

NICKY LYONS MYSTERY SERIES
ALL MINE (Book #1)
ALL HIS (Book #2)
ALL HE SEES (Book #3)
ALL ALONE (Book #4)

ALL FOR ONE (Book #5)
ALL HE TAKES (Book #6)
ALL FOR ME (Book #7)
ALL IN (Book #8)

CORA SHIELDS MYSTERY SERIES
UNDONE (Book #1)
UNWANTED (Book #2)
UNHINGED (Book #3)
UNSAID (Book #4)
UNGLUED (Book #5)
UNSTABLE (Book #6)
UNKNOWN (Book #7)
UNAWARE (Book #8)

MAY MOORE SUSPENSE THRILLER
NEVER RUN (Book #1)
NEVER TELL (Book #2)
NEVER LIVE (Book #3)
NEVER HIDE (Book #4)
NEVER FORGIVE (Book #5)
NEVER AGAIN (Book #6)
NEVER LOOK BACK (Book #7)
NEVER FORGET (Book #8)
NEVER LET GO (Book #9)
NEVER PRETEND (Book #10)
NEVER HESITATE (Book #11)

PAIGE KING MYSTERY SERIES
THE GIRL HE PINED (Book #1)
THE GIRL HE CHOSE (Book #2)
THE GIRL HE TOOK (Book #3)
THE GIRL HE WISHED (Book #4)
THE GIRL HE CROWNED (Book #5)
THE GIRL HE WATCHED (Book #6)
THE GIRL HE WANTED (Book #7)
THE GIRL HE CLAIMED (Book #8)

VALERIE LAW MYSTERY SERIES

NO MERCY (Book #1)
NO PITY (Book #2)
NO FEAR (Book #3)
NO SLEEP (Book #4)
NO QUARTER (Book #5)
NO CHANCE (Book #6)
NO REFUGE (Book #7)
NO GRACE (Book #8)
NO ESCAPE (Book #9)

RACHEL GIFT MYSTERY SERIES
HER LAST WISH (Book #1)
HER LAST CHANCE (Book #2)
HER LAST HOPE (Book #3)
HER LAST FEAR (Book #4)
HER LAST CHOICE (Book #5)
HER LAST BREATH (Book #6)
HER LAST MISTAKE (Book #7)
HER LAST DESIRE (Book #8)
HER LAST REGRET (Book #9)
HER LAST HOUR (Book #10)

AVA GOLD MYSTERY SERIES
CITY OF PREY (Book #1)
CITY OF FEAR (Book #2)
CITY OF BONES (Book #3)
CITY OF GHOSTS (Book #4)
CITY OF DEATH (Book #5)
CITY OF VICE (Book #6)

A YEAR IN EUROPE
A MURDER IN PARIS (Book #1)
DEATH IN FLORENCE (Book #2)
VENGEANCE IN VIENNA (Book #3)
A FATALITY IN SPAIN (Book #4)

ELLA DARK FBI SUSPENSE THRILLER
GIRL, ALONE (Book #1)
GIRL, TAKEN (Book #2)

GIRL, HUNTED (Book #3)
GIRL, SILENCED (Book #4)
GIRL, VANISHED (Book 5)
GIRL ERASED (Book #6)
GIRL, FORSAKEN (Book #7)
GIRL, TRAPPED (Book #8)
GIRL, EXPENDABLE (Book #9)
GIRL, ESCAPED (Book #10)
GIRL, HIS (Book #11)
GIRL, LURED (Book #12)
GIRL, MISSING (Book #13)
GIRL, UNKNOWN (Book #14)

LAURA FROST FBI SUSPENSE THRILLER
ALREADY GONE (Book #1)
ALREADY SEEN (Book #2)
ALREADY TRAPPED (Book #3)
ALREADY MISSING (Book #4)
ALREADY DEAD (Book #5)
ALREADY TAKEN (Book #6)
ALREADY CHOSEN (Book #7)
ALREADY LOST (Book #8)
ALREADY HIS (Book #9)
ALREADY LURED (Book #10)
ALREADY COLD (Book #11)

EUROPEAN VOYAGE COZY MYSTERY SERIES
MURDER (AND BAKLAVA) (Book #1)
DEATH (AND APPLE STRUDEL) (Book #2)
CRIME (AND LAGER) (Book #3)
MISFORTUNE (AND GOUDA) (Book #4)
CALAMITY (AND A DANISH) (Book #5)
MAYHEM (AND HERRING) (Book #6)

ADELE SHARP MYSTERY SERIES
LEFT TO DIE (Book #1)
LEFT TO RUN (Book #2)
LEFT TO HIDE (Book #3)
LEFT TO KILL (Book #4)

LEFT TO MURDER (Book #5)
LEFT TO ENVY (Book #6)
LEFT TO LAPSE (Book #7)
LEFT TO VANISH (Book #8)
LEFT TO HUNT (Book #9)
LEFT TO FEAR (Book #10)
LEFT TO PREY (Book #11)
LEFT TO LURE (Book #12)
LEFT TO CRAVE (Book #13)
LEFT TO LOATHE (Book #14)
LEFT TO HARM (Book #15)
LEFT TO RUIN (Book #16)

THE AU PAIR SERIES
ALMOST GONE (Book#1)
ALMOST LOST (Book #2)
ALMOST DEAD (Book #3)

ZOE PRIME MYSTERY SERIES
FACE OF DEATH (Book#1)
FACE OF MURDER (Book #2)
FACE OF FEAR (Book #3)
FACE OF MADNESS (Book #4)
FACE OF FURY (Book #5)
FACE OF DARKNESS (Book #6)

A JESSIE HUNT PSYCHOLOGICAL SUSPENSE SERIES
THE PERFECT WIFE (Book #1)
THE PERFECT BLOCK (Book #2)
THE PERFECT HOUSE (Book #3)
THE PERFECT SMILE (Book #4)
THE PERFECT LIE (Book #5)
THE PERFECT LOOK (Book #6)
THE PERFECT AFFAIR (Book #7)
THE PERFECT ALIBI (Book #8)
THE PERFECT NEIGHBOR (Book #9)
THE PERFECT DISGUISE (Book #10)
THE PERFECT SECRET (Book #11)
THE PERFECT FAÇADE (Book #12)

THE PERFECT IMPRESSION (Book #13)
THE PERFECT DECEIT (Book #14)
THE PERFECT MISTRESS (Book #15)
THE PERFECT IMAGE (Book #16)
THE PERFECT VEIL (Book #17)
THE PERFECT INDISCRETION (Book #18)
THE PERFECT RUMOR (Book #19)
THE PERFECT COUPLE (Book #20)
THE PERFECT MURDER (Book #21)
THE PERFECT HUSBAND (Book #22)
THE PERFECT SCANDAL (Book #23)
THE PERFECT MASK (Book #24)
THE PERFECT RUSE (Book #25)
THE PERFECT VENEER (Book #26)
THE PERFECT PEOPLE (Book #27)
THE PERFECT WITNESS (Book #28)

CHLOE FINE PSYCHOLOGICAL SUSPENSE SERIES
NEXT DOOR (Book #1)
A NEIGHBOR'S LIE (Book #2)
CUL DE SAC (Book #3)
SILENT NEIGHBOR (Book #4)
HOMECOMING (Book #5)
TINTED WINDOWS (Book #6)

KATE WISE MYSTERY SERIES
IF SHE KNEW (Book #1)
IF SHE SAW (Book #2)
IF SHE RAN (Book #3)
IF SHE HID (Book #4)
IF SHE FLED (Book #5)
IF SHE FEARED (Book #6)
IF SHE HEARD (Book #7)

THE MAKING OF RILEY PAIGE SERIES
WATCHING (Book #1)
WAITING (Book #2)
LURING (Book #3)
TAKING (Book #4)

STALKING (Book #5)
KILLING (Book #6)

RILEY PAIGE MYSTERY SERIES
ONCE GONE (Book #1)
ONCE TAKEN (Book #2)
ONCE CRAVED (Book #3)
ONCE LURED (Book #4)
ONCE HUNTED (Book #5)
ONCE PINED (Book #6)
ONCE FORSAKEN (Book #7)
ONCE COLD (Book #8)
ONCE STALKED (Book #9)
ONCE LOST (Book #10)
ONCE BURIED (Book #11)
ONCE BOUND (Book #12)
ONCE TRAPPED (Book #13)
ONCE DORMANT (Book #14)
ONCE SHUNNED (Book #15)
ONCE MISSED (Book #16)
ONCE CHOSEN (Book #17)

MACKENZIE WHITE MYSTERY SERIES
BEFORE HE KILLS (Book #1)
BEFORE HE SEES (Book #2)
BEFORE HE COVETS (Book #3)
BEFORE HE TAKES (Book #4)
BEFORE HE NEEDS (Book #5)
BEFORE HE FEELS (Book #6)
BEFORE HE SINS (Book #7)
BEFORE HE HUNTS (Book #8)
BEFORE HE PREYS (Book #9)
BEFORE HE LONGS (Book #10)
BEFORE HE LAPSES (Book #11)
BEFORE HE ENVIES (Book #12)
BEFORE HE STALKS (Book #13)
BEFORE HE HARMS (Book #14)

AVERY BLACK MYSTERY SERIES

CAUSE TO KILL (Book #1)
CAUSE TO RUN (Book #2)
CAUSE TO HIDE (Book #3)
CAUSE TO FEAR (Book #4)
CAUSE TO SAVE (Book #5)
CAUSE TO DREAD (Book #6)

KERI LOCKE MYSTERY SERIES
A TRACE OF DEATH (Book #1)
A TRACE OF MURDER (Book #2)
A TRACE OF VICE (Book #3)
A TRACE OF CRIME (Book #4)
A TRACE OF HOPE (Book #5)

PROLOGUE

The endless hedges towered in front of her, blocking out the sun and casting deep shadows on the ground. They seemed to go on forever in all directions, with no end in sight. The quiet, almost eerie silence was pierced by the occasional rustling of leaves, the distant music from the theme park, and the sound of her own footsteps echoing through the dirt. How big was this maze supposed to be? Marcy had to admit that it was suffocating her.

She dashed forward, hoping to see any sign of her friends. One minute, they'd all been together, and now, she was alone. Marcy’s nostrils filled with the pungent scent of the overgrown shrubs, but the smell of popcorn and cotton candy that wafted through the air reminded her that she was still in an amusement park—lost as she was, she'd find her way out.

Right?

Marcy's heart was pounding in her chest, and sweat trickled down her forehead. Every turn she took seemed to lead to another dead end. What had started out as simple frustration was now causing her anxiety to peak. Panic was quickly setting in as she realized she had no idea how long she had been wandering aimlessly, lost within the maze. Was it hours? Minutes? She couldn't tell, but her panic attack grew more intense by the moment. It reminded her of when she was little, and she’d lost her parents in the mall for hours, and a stranger had nearly tried to take her home before security found her. It had been so long, but her therapist had told her that childhood trauma could keep rearing its ugly head as an adult, and that her panic attacks could be attributed to that.

You’re fine, she tried to tell herself, *it’s going to be okay!* But her mind was still swimming with anxious thoughts.

Suddenly, Marcy stumbled. Her ankle twisted over a root, and she cried out, falling to the ground. Pain shot through her leg, but she gritted her teeth and stood up, trying to put weight on it. She hissed in pain, and she knew she wouldn't be able to make it on her own. She needed help.

"Guys?" Marcy called out, her voice cracking with fear. "Anyone?"

There was no answer, and Marcy felt her heart drop. She was all alone in the maze. Her friends had ditched her.

The pain dulled. When Marcy was sure she could walk, she stood up. It wasn't so bad. She kept pushing forward, and forward, until—

Marcy screamed as she crashed right into someone else. She fell backwards, landing on her butt in the dirt.

Then, laughter. Marcy looked up to see her best friends, Julie and Kat, looking down at her.

"Oh my god, there you are!" Julie exclaimed.

Marcy scowled as she stood up and dusted herself off, her ankle still tender. She glowered at her friends. "Where did you guys go? You left me all alone!"

"We got lost!" Kat said, grinning. "We were wandering around, and suddenly, we found ourselves in a completely different section of the maze. We tried to retrace our steps, but we couldn't find you."

Marcy rolled her eyes, but relief flooded through her as she realized she wasn't alone anymore. "Well, let's get out of here before I get lost again."

The three of them started to walk, but their progress was slow. The hedges seemed to be growing thicker and more tangled the farther they went, and Marcy's ankle made it difficult to keep up with the others. But they kept pushing forward, determined to find the exit. Marcy kept her guard up as they navigated the maze. They turned and a corner, and—

An ear-splitting scream erupted from Kat's throat.

Marcy jumped back, her heart pounding. At first, she thought it was another prank.

"What the hell, Kat?" she yelled, but then she saw it too.

Up ahead, half-buried in the dirt, was the upper torso of a woman, adorned with flowers like some sort of scarecrow. Relief flowed through Marcy.

"Oh my God, Kat, it's just a freaking prop," Marcy said.

But then, as she got closer, her relief was replaced by dread. The woman's eyes were open and glassy. Her skin was pale and waxy. Marcy could feel the bile rising in her throat as she realized what she was seeing—it wasn't a scarecrow at all.

It was a real dead body.

All three girls screamed and ran for their lives.

CHAPTER ONE

Morgan Cross pulled her weight up, feeling her muscles burn as she performed another pull-up—twenty consecutively in a row. It was a habit she'd picked up in prison, back when she'd been wrongfully convicted, but it was one of the good habits. Not like biting her nails, which she'd developed as she'd sat in that cold cell for ten years, anxiously waiting for the day she'd be released.

But that was in the past now. She was free, and she was here—back with the FBI. She'd installed the pull-up bar in her office. It made it feel a bit more like home.

A knock on the wall beyond her door broke her thoughts. Morgan dropped down, sweat pooling at her hairline. She found herself face-to-face with Derik Greene's blue eyes. He lifted a curious brow, and Morgan said, "What?" as she grabbed a towel off her chair and wiped her forehead, then pivoted behind her desk.

"You're looking strong," Derik noted. They'd been partners before Morgan went away, and now, they were back together again. His dark hair was combed to the side, and he had a curious expression on as he stepped deeper into Morgan's office. Even though they'd worked on one case together since she got out, she couldn't help but still think about ten years ago when they'd shared a kiss. When Derik was still married.

It had been a long time since then, she reminded herself.

Things were different now.

"Something I can help you with, Greene?" she asked him, sitting down with a huff.

He tossed a newspaper on her desk. Morgan inched it closer to her, taking in the front headline:

MAZE KILLER STILL AT LARGE.

And another newspaper.

POLICE AT DEAD END IN MAZE KILLER CASE.

And one more.

MAZE KILLER CLAIMS ANOTHER VICTIM. DANGER TO PUBLIC GROWING!

And—

"Okay, I get it," Morgan said, lifting a hand to stop Derik from throwing another newspaper on her desk. "So, what gives? Are the locals finally gonna get us in to help them?" Generally speaking, the police would not let the FBI do their jobs, only come in if needed or requested. Morgan had heard about this case—this alleged "Maze Killer" who was leaving dead bodies in mazes, with a completely sterile scene, not a speck of DNA.

"Not yet," Derik said, "but it shouldn't be long before we start to poke around, don't you think?"

Morgan stood up. The old her would have been all over this, and maybe it did pique her interest. But things were different now. She'd become jaded in her time in prison, and she'd lost the desire to force herself into situations where she wasn't requested. It was up to the local PD, after all, if they wanted to come to the FBI for help.

Then again, this wasn't about her. There were real people out there, losing their lives.

Still, they hadn't been called.

Morgan picked up her phone, then shot AD Mueller a text: *Maze Killer is getting bad?*

When she looked up from her phone, Derik was staring at her. "There," she said, "let's see what Mueller thinks. It's the best we can do for now. You want to grab lunch?"

Derik nodded, and they headed out of the office, the headlines still weighing heavily on Morgan's mind. She couldn't help but wonder what kind of sick person would do something like this. The thought made her stomach churn with disgust, and part of her did hope she'd be given the chance to take a crack at this case. After all, she was just getting her chops back. Her time in prison hadn't made her weaker—it made her stronger. More resolute.

If given the chance, she'd put that bastard right where he belonged.

***

Morgan slid into the booth, the sun streaming in from the windows, even with the dark and stormy rain clouds rolling in. Still, it wasn't storming yet, and everything seemed bathed in a soft warmth. Derik sat across from her. It had been hard to come out of prison and fall back into her old routine, but she had to admit that Derik had been a welcome addition. They had history, to say the least.

"So, bacon and eggs?" Derik asked, skimming through the laminated menu. Morgan's usual diner order.

But as she was about to grab the menu, the TV above the counter caught her eye. On it was a giant headline: MAZE KILLER. She didn't signal to Derik, just tuned her ears to the people sitting below the TV, watching, as they said:

"I can't believe anyone would go in some maze at a time like this."

Another person chimed in. "I heard that he's been doing this for a while, but no one ever caught on. Now, he's just getting bolder."

A sense of unease washed over her. This wasn't just some run-of-the-mill serial killer. This was someone who was taunting the police, daring them to catch him with his brazen and bold acts. It had to be a statement. And so far, the police had no luck.

Derik seemed to notice the conversation, too, as he lifted an eyebrow at Morgan over his menu. The truth was, the case was starting to get under her skin.

Derik nodded, as if he understood the unspoken message. "Well, if we do get called in, I'm all for taking this guy down."

Morgan quietly agreed.

After their food was delivered, Derik made conversation as he took bites of his cut-up back bacon. Morgan ate her bacon and eggs, trying not to show her inner protective nature over her food that had grown over the past ten years, back from when she was locked up and her portions had been rationed.

"So, how are you settling back into work?" Derik asked.

Morgan paused, fork frozen in midair. She hadn't really thought about it. Work had been a welcome distraction, but it was hard to ignore the fact that she was now back in a world that had moved on without her. "It's been an adjustment. You know how it is." She took a sip of her coffee, letting the warmth spread through her. "But it feels good to be back in the field again. Like I'm doing something important."

Derik nodded, his gaze flickering up to the TV above them. Morgan followed his line of sight, watching as the news anchor spoke somberly about the latest victim of the Maze Killer. A shiver ran down her spine, but she forced herself to push it aside.

"Yeah, I can imagine," Derik said. "But hey, for what it's worth, you're doing great, Morgan. You always were one of the best."

Morgan gave a small smile, grateful for the words of encouragement, but they also left a bitter taste on her tongue. She was one of the best, and yet she'd been sent to prison and lost ten precious years of her life, all over something she never did.

Then again, it wasn't Derik's fault. There were a lot of people to blame for what happened to her, but at least he was waiting with a friendly smile after everything. Still, she wished he'd had her back more, that he'd fought more to keep her free. She knew he'd tried to testify to her innocence, but it was out of Derik's hands too. Morgan knew that.

She had thought about him a lot in prison, wondering if he still thought about her, if his trust in her ever wavered. It was true that people had been divided on Morgan's guilt; some thought she had assisted a serial killer, Samson—the Seven Signs Killer—in his crimes, but Derik always maintained her innocence.

Still, after many years, it seemed he'd given up on her, too, before she was released. He did visit her in prison, but as far as trying to get her out … that had dulled down.

She couldn't blame him. It wasn't his job or responsibility. A lot of what happened to her was on Assistant Director Mueller, if anyone, because he hadn't believed her even though he was supposed to be on her side. She'd been bumping heads with him since she got out, even though he'd wanted her on the most recent Seven Signs case with Derik. He'd offered her a contract to come back, but after a massive break, in which Deputy Director Irvin had gone over his head and brought Morgan back early.

It had only been a week since then, and Morgan was settling in well enough, even though she felt hostility from Mueller whenever she had to cross him in the hall.

"Thanks, D," Morgan said, realizing she never addressed Derik's compliment.

They finished their meal and headed back out. As they stepped out into the bright sunlight, Morgan couldn't help but reflect on how much she'd missed. Ten years of her dog, Skunk's, life—that was one of the most painful parts. Skunk was old now, and Morgan had missed most of it. Her father used to show her pictures when he'd visit weekly, before he died, not long before Morgan's release. Morgan's neighbor,

Lora, had returned Skunk to her, claiming Skunk hadn't been the same since Morgan got back, and he clearly wanted to be with her. Skunk was at home with Morgan now, but the regret still weighed on her. She wished things were different, but they weren't.

They got back to HQ and went inside, but as soon as they reached their office area, the intern, Maggie, ran right up to them with her eyes bulging out.

"Oh, thank God I found you!" she exclaimed.

Morgan lifted a brow. "What is it?"

"I need you two to come with me now," Maggie said. "We got a message from the Maze Killer—and it's addressed to us."

Morgan's stomach dropped, and she exchanged a look with Derik. "To the FBI?" Morgan clarified.

"Yes!" Maggie exclaimed. "Come on, come quick."

Morgan and Derik followed Maggie to a conference room where a team had already assembled, their faces tense as they stared at a laptop screen displaying a message from the Maze Killer. Morgan could feel the adrenaline pumping through her veins as she read the message, her heart racing with excitement and fear.

Hello, Dear FBI,

The police are too incompetent. Think you can do better?

My next victim is out there—you can still save her ...

If you make it in time!

Come to the maze at the governor's estate.

You have less than one hour.

Then, she dies.

Your move, FBI.

Morgan's heart raced as she read the note, processing it, partially feeling like it was a joke.

But it wasn't. It was real.

Morgan felt a chill run down her spine. This was no ordinary killer. This was someone who was proud of their work and wanted to show off. She wondered what kind of sick game the Maze Killer was playing.

"Okay," Morgan said, breaking the silence. "We need to trace this email. Special Agent Greene and I will head to the scene. The rest of you—work on finding out everything you can about the sender."

Everyone in the room nodded in agreement, and Morgan made her way to the door with Derik right behind her. As they walked through the hallway, she could feel her heart pounding in her chest. This was the moment she had been waiting for. Ten years of thinking about all the things she couldn't do, and now, she was going to be able to do something that mattered. Something that could save a life.

As they made their way to the governor's estate, Morgan couldn't help but think about the last time she had been in a situation like this. The last time she had received a taunting message from a killer, and how it had almost cost her everything. But this time, things were different. This time, she was prepared. She was ready.

CHAPTER TWO

Rain poured violently over the estate. Morgan arrived at the scene in record time, the flashing lights of police cars blinding as she pulled her car up to the gate. Morgan and Derik jumped out of the vehicle and were instantly drenched—cold rain made the goosebumps on Morgan's arms raise and her clothes stick to her skin, but she pushed on. They were met by a swarm of police officers, all trying to figure out what was going on. A helicopter was parked off to the side, standing by for aerial support.

"Where's the maze?" Morgan demanded at an officer, her voice cold and commanding as she flashed her badge. The sound of the rain was deafening; it was a constant roar in the background, like a symphony playing in reverse.

"This way." The lead officer pointed in the direction of a large hedge maze that had been set up in the backyard of the governor's estate. "Over there," he said.

Morgan looked into the abyss of the maze, then glanced back at Derik. She nodded at him. "You take the sky, I'll lead the ground team in."

Derik nodded. "Good luck." With that, he jogged in the rain toward the helicopter to meet with the team.

Morgan refocused on the officer. She knew she had to stay focused, no matter what they might find in that maze. "I need to speak with whomever is in charge of the operation."

The officer pointed to a figure in a slicker and hat, pacing back and forth in front of the entrance to the maze. Morgan marched over to him, the rain almost blinding her. She could hear the sound of her footsteps pounding against the soaked grass.

"Special Agent Morgan Cross," she said, introducing herself, "what's the situation?"

The man in charge turned toward her, his face haggard and tired. "We've been searching for the victim for about thirty minutes now, but we haven't found anything. We're moving as quickly as we can."

Thirty minutes. By the time the email had been sent, there had only been an hour left on the clock. Now, it was cut in half. They needed to act fast.

"What's the layout of the maze?" Morgan asked. "Do you have a map?"

The officer nodded, handing over a piece of paper with a crudely drawn map of the maze. Morgan studied it quickly, trying to memorize the twists and turns. She took a deep breath, her heart pounding in her chest. This was it. This was what she had been trained for. After so many years locked up, she had to admit that it felt good to get her hands dirty again.

Still, her nerves grew. There was always the risk of failure. And she didn't want another body on her conscience.

"Okay," she said. "I'm going in. Special Agent Greene will be handling the aerial search."

The person nodded, and Morgan took off into the maze, her feet splashing through the puddles that had formed. A sense of foreboding washed over her as she ran. The rain made it hard to see, and she could hear the sound of crunching leaves and twigs underfoot. The maze was labyrinthine, with twists and turns that seemed to go on forever.

It was quiet, too quiet, as if the rain had washed away any sound that might have been there before. Above, the rotaries of the helicopter spun as it soared over the maze, a spotlight on the ground, searching for any sign of this alleged victim.

Morgan kept running and searching, but despite her thoroughness, she found nothing. The rain kept pummeling her, and the maze seemed to go on forever. She was cold and exhausted, but she knew she had to keep going. Someone out here needed her—needed to be saved.

She turned a corner and came face-to-face with a wall, her heart racing as she realized she had hit a dead end. She looked at the map again, trying to figure out where she had gone wrong. She retraced her steps, trying to find where she had taken a wrong turn. The helicopter swooped above again.

Time was running out. Morgan's lungs heaved, and the rain kept pouring. The weather caused an assault of memories to flit through her mind. When she was in prison, there were many rainy days that had passed beyond the bars of her cell window. She remembered her bitterness, her resentment, her pointless wishes to be let go, to be seen as innocent.

And yet none of that ever happened. Ten years behind bars can change a person.

Morgan shook her head, clearing the memories away. Ten years was enough. She had to focus on the task at hand; she couldn't let that person out in the maze go unprotected. She kept running, checking every corner and crevice for any sign of life, but she saw nothing.

The seconds ticked away, and Morgan could feel the frustration building up inside her chest. She had to find this person, she had to save them from whatever danger lurked within these walls. She clenched her jaw and started running faster and faster, determined not to fail again.

As she turned a corner, she saw a figure in the distance. It was a person, lying on the ground. Morgan's heart jumped in her chest, and she raced toward the figure, her feet slipping in the mud, her hair whipping in the wind.

But the closer she got, the more apparent it became.

Half-buried in the ground was the upper half of a woman's torso, her red hair matted and bloody. Morgan collapsed in front of the woman. She already knew the truth.

They were too late.

Morgan turned around to see the front of the woman. Her eyes were open and lifeless, her cheeks barely flushed from the life that had only recently flowed through her.

They were too late.

Numb, Morgan took out her phone. Rain drops splashed against the screen as she called Derik. He answered right away.

"Cross—"

"Call it off," Morgan said.

"What?"

"I said call it off, Derik. I found her."

"Is she ..."

Derik trailed off, likely already knowing the answer based off Morgan's silence.

"Okay," Derek conceded. "Let's call it off."

Morgan hung up the phone and sat there for a moment, feeling the rain as it pelted her from above. She felt helpless, like she had failed. This was not the outcome she had hoped for. But it was too late now.

Maybe all of this was a trick, a diversion tactic of some kind. Maybe there was never any hope of finding this young woman alive.

Morgan stood up, her eyes fixed on the lifeless body of the victim. She felt a sense of failure wash over her. They were too late to save this woman. She wondered how many more would be taken before they caught the Maze Killer.

A sense of anger took over her. This was personal now. The killer had called the FBI here directly, taunted them, dangling this woman's life over their noses, and Morgan couldn't let that slide. It was as if the killer wasn't satisfied by the police's incompetence, so he wanted more of a challenge. As if people's lives were simply a game to him.

Morgan took a deep breath, wiping the rain from her face. She had to keep her emotions under control, had to stay focused on the task at hand. She couldn't let the anger consume her, not now, not when they were so close. She had to find a way to stop the Maze Killer, to end this madness once and for all. Morgan knew that the only way to catch this sick and twisted individual was to get inside his mind. She had to think like him, to understand what made him tick. It wasn't going to be easy, but he'd made a mistake by choosing to mess with the FBI.

"Cross!" a voice called, and Morgan turned to see Derik rushing up with a crew of officers. The rain lightened, but the damage had been done to the crime scene. Like the last one, Morgan was sure they'd find nothing.

"Hey." Morgan nodded at Derik.

His face darkened as he walked up to the body. "We couldn't save her," Derik said, his voice low and filled with regret.

Morgan nodded slowly, her eyes fixed on the victim's face. She felt a deep sadness wash over her, a feeling of loss that she couldn't quite shake off. This woman had been someone's daughter, someone's friend, someone's sister. And now, she was gone, taken by a killer who seemed to relish in the pain and suffering of others.

"We need to catch this guy," Morgan said firmly, her jaw clenched.

Derik nodded, his eyes burning with determination. "We will," he said. "In the meantime"—he gestured to the officers around him—"let's get this scene extracted. We need all the forensic evidence we can get."

Morgan watched as the officers moved around the crime scene, snapping photos and collecting evidence. She couldn't help but feel a sense of helplessness wash over her as she realized how little they had to go on. The Maze Killer was cunning, and he seemed to always be one step ahead of them.

But Morgan refused to give up. She'd spent ten years in prison, and she'd survived it.

She could survive this too.

Just then, a voice boomed over the sound of officers' voices and the rain. "Let me through, let me through!" A man pushed his way through the crowd.

The governor.

This was his estate, after all, and the officers had clearly failed to keep him out of the maze. A small, mousy officer tried to hold him back, but he pushed his way through. The governor was a tall man, towering over the other officers at the scene. His hair, a mix of salt and pepper, was cut short and neatly styled. He had a strong jawline and piercing eyes that surveyed the situation with authority. His posture was authoritative, and his presence commanded attention.

"Sir, please, you shouldn't—" the officer began, but the governor's eyes had already fallen on the dead body half-buried in his garden maze. His face went pale, but only for a moment. He looked right at Morgan and Derik; unlike the other officers on the scene, they were dressed in basic black, and he must have sensed they were the FBI agents in charge.

"Do you have any idea how big of a scandal this could be for me?" the governor asked.

Morgan glowered. This was what he cared about at a time like this? "A woman is dead on your property, governor."

The governor's eyes narrowed at Morgan's tone, but she held his gaze firmly.

"I know you," he said, and Morgan's jaw clenched. "You're that criminal FBI agent."

Morgan's blood burned at his words. "I was exonerated, sir," she said. And if he really watched the news, he'd know that most of the media had taken Morgan's side. But that didn't change the reality that there would always be people who looked at her like she was a criminal.

The governor peered at Morgan, his eyes narrowing. "I don't care what the media says. You were locked up for a reason."

Morgan resisted the urge to roll her eyes. "With all due respect, sir, I don't think that's what we should be focusing on right now. We need to catch the Maze Killer, and fast."

The governor shook his head, his eyes fixed on the victim's body. "This is a disaster," he muttered. "A complete and utter disaster. I can't have this kind of negative publicity on my property."

Morgan gritted her teeth, struggling to keep her anger in check. "I think you're missing the point here, sir. A woman is dead. We need to find her killer. That's all that matters right now."

"I understand that, Agent Cross, but I have a reputation to uphold here. Do you understand me?"

Morgan took a deep breath, fighting to keep her voice even. "I understand, sir. But right now, we need your full cooperation if we're going to catch the Maze Killer."

"I understand that, Agent Cross," he said slowly. "But this is my property, and I need to know that this won't become a media circus."

Morgan gritted her teeth, but before she could respond, Derik stepped in.

"Governor, we're doing everything we can to catch the killer," he said firmly. "But right now, our priority is to collect all the evidence we can. We need your cooperation to do that."

The governor hesitated but eventually nodded. "Fine. But I want to be kept in the loop about what's happening here," he said. "I don't want any surprises, and I don't want cameras here. You got that?"

Morgan exchanged a glance with Derik. As if they didn't have enough on their plate already with the Maze Killer, now they had to deal with a politician who cared more about his reputation than the dead woman in his garden. But all they could do was nod and agree to keep him informed.

Morgan gritted her teeth, staring back at the body as the governor took off. Good riddance; Morgan could think more without him breathing down her neck.

She approached the body, noting how much effort the killer had put in to half-bury her like this. They weren't dealing with a simple killer here, that much was obvious. This man had an agenda, and he wanted attention. The Maze Killer was getting bolder and more twisted with each new victim, and they needed to stop him before he struck again. She wondered what kind of man would go to this much trouble to be so theatrical. He must have been a lonely person, an attention-seeking person, maybe with some sort of personality disorder that remanded attention, although that was purely speculative. She tried to build up an image in her mind of who he could be; a middle-aged man, probably someone who had been rejected by society and was now taking his revenge on it. Or maybe he was a younger man, someone who had been deeply traumatized in his childhood and was now acting out his pain on other people. Morgan couldn't be sure, but she knew that they needed to catch him fast. They had to find a way to get inside the killer's mind, to understand his motives and his methods.

Right now, only one thing was certain: based on the Maze Killer's track record, the next body to drop would be in another maze entirely.

Morgan clenched her teeth, eyes lingering on the body of the victim.

Not if I find you first.

CHAPTER THREE

Back at HQ, Morgan looked down at her desk as Derik slapped another stack of papers down. She looked up at him, raising an eyebrow, but Derik's face was completely unfazed.

"Really?" Morgan asked, shoving the paperwork aside. She focused back on her computer, taking in the screen in front of her. She was in the middle of learning everything she could about the Maze Killer and would rather not break her concentration. "Can't you deal with the paperwork?" she asked.

Derik sighed and sat down. "We both need to sign off on some of these," he said. "It'll only take a sec."

Morgan rolled her eyes but grabbed the stack of papers and began signing where needed. As she went through the paperwork, her mind couldn't help but drift back to the case. She wasn't sure how this guy was pulling off these crimes—killing these women and burying them so publicly and not getting caught at all or leaving any shred of DNA. The Maze Killer was too good, too careful.

Frustration rinsed over her. They were running out of time. How many more women would have to die before they caught him? She knew that they needed a breakthrough, something that would give them an edge in the case. They needed to get ahead of the Maze Killer.

"There." Morgan handed the papers back to Derik. He stood up, gripping them, but then hesitated to leave. Morgan looked up at him; she could tell he wanted to say more.

"What have you learned?" he asked.

She let out a sigh. "Well, so far, this guy has killed four women. Really, the case should've gone to us after the second, before the media storm, but we can't change that now."

"Agreed," Derik said. "I wish we'd had our eye on it sooner, but we were busy."

Busy. That was an understatement. Morgan had been swept right back into the case of the Seven Signs killer when she got out of prison, so she hadn't exactly been on the hunt for other serial killers to track down.

But the Maze Killer's timeline had unfolded rapidly. Four women in the past month, and the last two were the closest together. That was an aggressive timeline, and Morgan was sure it was only the beginning.

Most notably, though, was that the killer clearly had a type. All the women were in their mid to late thirties, red-haired, and were killed with blunt force trauma to the back of the head—a fairly clean hit that did the job quick. That aside, the crime scenes became so messy because of the way he buried them, which caused blood to get everywhere. And yet not a speck of the actual killer's DNA—at least not yet—had been found.

"Why do you think he's going after red-haired women in their thirties?" Morgan asked, hoping to pick Derik's brain.

He eased back into the seat, letting out a breath. "Let's see here ... maybe he's pissed off at a wife? A mother? Sister? Ex-lover?"

Morgan considered this for a moment. "It's possible. Maybe it's a twisted fantasy he has. Maybe he's hurting women who look like someone in his life."

Derik nodded. "That's definitely another possibility. We won't know for sure until we catch him. The pool of red-haired women in the city is, well, broad."

Morgan leaned back in her chair, running a hand over her face. "God, I hate this feeling of being so helpless. Every lead the cops have followed have led nowhere."

Derik offered a smile. "Hey, don't get discouraged yet. We're in this now. It's in our hands."

She smiled faintly at him, grateful for his support. In the midst of all the chaos and frustration of the case, she was glad to have someone like Derik by her side. But she had to admit that the fear of getting it wrong was still present in her.

"You remember back in the day?" Derik suddenly said, and Morgan lifted a brow. It still felt weird to talk about the past with Derik, after she'd been out of the picture for ten long years behind bars for a wrongful conviction.

"What about back in the day?" she asked.

"We tackled some of the toughest cases out there," Derik said. "You were always one of our best, and I was honored to work with you."

Morgan turned away, her face warming with embarrassment. Reconnecting with Derik after so long wasn't a walk in the park. She felt awkward sometimes, other times a little resentful. He might not have put her behind bars, but he didn't get her out, either.

Still, he was right. They had history in the FBI. They'd cracked some of the hardest cases in the history of the Bureau, and they had cracked them open together. It had been a time of great success and accomplishment, before everything had gone wrong with her conviction.

"Yeah, those were some good times," she said, a wistful smile tugging at the corner of her mouth.

Derik grinned. "We can have those times again. We just need to catch this guy, put him away, and move on to the next case. It's what we do."

"It's what you did for ten years while I was locked up," Morgan corrected. She hadn't meant to come across so bitter, but she couldn't help it.

Derik's expression fell. "I know," he said softly. "And I'm sorry. I should've done more."

Morgan shook her head, trying to push the feelings of resentment aside. "It's not your fault, Derik. You at least tried to testify for me."

"But it wasn't enough. And … I guess, eventually, I gave up."

Her heart sank, his words only confirming what she knew to be true. It hurt, she had to admit, but what good would getting angry do? Even though Morgan knew that if the same thing had happened to Derik, she never would have stopped fighting for him. "It wasn't your job," she said.

Silence hung between them for a few moments before Derik spoke up again. "Listen, Morgan," he said, his tone serious, "I know you're still adjusting to life outside of prison, but I want you to know that I've got your back. Whatever you need, I'm here for you."

Morgan felt a pang of guilt at her earlier bitterness. Derik had always been a good friend, even if she had been too stubborn to see it at times. "Thanks," she said softly. "It means a lot."

"I'm gonna go send this in," Derik said, holding up the paperwork. "Let's reconvene in a bit."

She nodded, and Derik left the room.

Morgan leaned back in her chair, trying to clear her mind. She needed to think about this case from a different angle, to see if there was anything they'd missed. She thought back to the timeline the killer had given them. If the victim had been alive when they'd started looking—which, according to the crime scene, it did seem like the kill was fairly fresh—then that would mean that if the blunt force trauma was what killed her, then the killer would have had to be present just moments before Morgan found the woman dead. Was that even possible? There was no way he could have escaped with all those officers and the helicopter in the sky. Someone would have seen him.

Just then, her phone rang on her desk. Morgan quickly swiped it up.

"This is Morgan Cross."

"Special Agent Cross?" a tentative voice said. "It's Amy from forensics. I ... I think you need to see something."

Morgan sat up, her heart racing. Maybe this was it—the one thing they needed to take the killer down. Their golden ticket.

"I'll be right there," Morgan said, then hung up and sped out of the room.

***

Morgan stood behind Amy, the forensic analyst, in front of a computer screen as Amy showed the toxicology results from the two previous victims. There had been a short break between the first two, but the last two had been killed within a couple days of each other.

"Check this out," Amy said. "The last victim, Mia Jones—the girl found in the amusement park maze—had trace amounts of a specific kind of poison in her bloodstream."

"What?" Morgan's heart sank. This hadn't been in the file.

"It's a recent find," Amy clarified. "It almost went undetected. We think she was force fed a high concentration of leaves from a Bleeding Woodbine, which is a type of plant with berries and leaves that are very toxic to humans. Normally, toxicity can take a while to be fatal, but if given a high enough amount, it could kill within an hour. We're checking to see if we can find it in our most current victim too."

The current victim. Right. The woman Morgan had found at the governor's estate. Grace Alba, thirty-four. She had a name. A life. A family. A husband. A—

"But that's not all I wanted to show you," Amy said. "Look."

Morgan focused on the screen. On it were pictures of Grace's autopsy. There were bruises along her arms.

"We didn’t see this type of bruising on any of the other victims," Amy clarified. "We're wondering if Grace already had the bruises when she died."

Morgan frowned. If it wasn't the killer who'd bruised Grace, then who?

"She had a husband," Morgan said.

Amy nodded, tight-lipped. "We can't say who did it for sure, but the bruises seem to be older."

Morgan's mind raced, connecting the dots as she thought about the latest victim's husband. Could he have been the Maze Killer all along? Was it possible that he was so cunning that he'd been able to disappear without a trace every time one of the murders took place?

But then again, why would he kill his own wife, after all the other girls? Maybe he was chasing the fantasy with the first three, then finished it off with the real thing.

"Can you run another check on this poison, see if it's in Grace?" Morgan asked, still staring at the photo of Grace's bruised arms.

Amy nodded. "We're already on it."

Morgan took a deep breath, her mind racing with possibilities. She needed to keep her cool, to think logically and rationally. "Okay. Thank you, Amy. Keep me posted on any updates."

As she walked out of the lab, Morgan's mind continued to spin. The fact that the latest victim's husband might have been the one to bruise her arms was a strange coincidence. Was it a coincidence at all?

She needed to talk to him. She needed to find out more about their relationship, their history. Maybe there was something there that could give them a clue about the killer's motive.

And she would. But one other thing concerned her, and that was the fact that if what Amy was saying about the poison was true, then that meant the girls really were already dead before they even had a chance to find them.

When the killer sent the FBI that note, it was already too late.

If that were true, then that meant the next victim—wherever she was, whoever she was—might already be beyond saving.

CHAPTER FOUR

The toxicology reports confirmed it: Grace Alba had been poisoned, the same way the other women had.

Sitting in the conference room at HQ with Derik, Morgan worked through every file the police had on the previous victims—and everything they were learning about their latest. All of these victims had things in common. For one, their red hair. Two, their age, mid to late thirties. The manner in which their bodies were found suggested the killer was an able-bodied male. The botany aspect also added another layer to the killer's potential profile. The Bleeding Woodbine poison found, so far, in each victim.

"According to the database," Morgan said, getting Derik's attention, "Grace's husband, Jim, works as a construction worker. Think he'd have the knowledge and access to the Bleeding Woodbine?"

Derik shrugged. "It's possible, but it could also be a coincidence. We don't know if Jim had any interest in botany or if he had access to the plant."

Morgan sighed, frustrated. She wished they had more concrete evidence to go off of. The fact that they were still grasping at straws made her feel uneasy. They needed to be methodical, to gather evidence and build a case against the killer brick by brick. But the sense of urgency was weighing heavily on her, knowing that they could be running out of time to save the next victim if they didn't act fast.

"We could be looking for a chemist with a unique knowledge of plants," Derik pointed out.

"A horticulturist, maybe," Morgan agreed. There could be a lot of different motives for someone to commit such heinous crimes, but the choice of poison seemed like it could tell them everything, if they knew where to look.

She looked at the photo of Grace's autopsy, spread out on the table before her. She slid it closer to her to get a better look at the bruises. She didn't want to draw any conclusions, but if Grace Alba's husband was abusive toward her, then he might fit the bill; a bitter, deranged husband, looking to enact revenge on his wife, playing out fantasies until he took the real deal. Morgan had seen a lot of domestic abuse cases in her day, and those bruises on Grace looked a lot like marks from an angry husband.

"What do you think about the husband?" Morgan asked Derik.

"I don't know, Morgan. It's still too early to point fingers," Derik replied. "We need more evidence before we can make any accusations."

Morgan nodded, but the nagging feeling in her gut wouldn't go away. She knew they had to tread carefully, but they couldn't ignore the possibility that Grace's husband could be the killer.

Morgan grabbed her laptop and went into the FBI database, looking into Jim Alba. Real name: James Timothy Alba, age thirty-eight. No criminal record. Worked for a construction company and made a good salary doing it. He'd married Grace ten years ago. Grace, on the other hand, worked as a school teacher. They had one child, eight years old.

That was another thing the victims all had in common. They had children.

Morgan focused on Jim's file. His bank statements could help build a picture of what he'd been up to the past few days, maybe show if he'd been anywhere near where the killings happened. They had the amusement park killing, then, more recently, the governor's estate.

Morgan looked through Jim's bank statements. Jim had made a large withdrawal from his account a few days before Grace's murder. The amount was in the thousands, and it seemed unusual for someone like Jim, who didn't have a history of making large withdrawals.

She kept scrolling. On the day Mia had been killed at the amusement park, Jim had apparently gone to a motel. Assuming he was alone, and Grace wasn't with him, then he might not have an alibi for that night at all.

Morgan continued on, but one transaction from the following day made her pause.

A charge at a gas station near the amusement park, the day after Mia was found.

She could feel her heart pounding in her chest as she realized that Jim Alba might actually be the Maze Killer.

She looked over at Derik, who was going over the autopsy reports. "Derik," she said, her voice shaking slightly, "I think we need to bring Jim Alba in for questioning."

Derik looked up at her, his expression wary. "Why? What do you have?"

Morgan hesitated for a moment, trying to gather her thoughts. "I found some charges on his bank statements near the locations of the other victims. And ... I have a feeling about him. I think he might be the killer."

Derik leaned back in his chair, studying her carefully. "You always did have top-notch intuition."

"Let's bring him in for questioning," Morgan said, standing up. "I want to know everything about their relationship, their history."

"You really think it could be him?" Derik asked, standing up. "Why would he kill three separate women before his own wife?"

"Some sort of murder fantasy until he took the real thing, obviously," Morgan said. "Just because a killer starts with non-related victims, doesn't mean they won't eventually target someone close to them. Maybe he was working up to it, or maybe Grace discovered something about him, and he had to silence her. But there must be a reason why he chose these women. They all have red hair, they're all around the same age, and they all have children. It's possible that he has some sort of grudge against women with these characteristics. Such as his wife."

Derik nodded. "Alright, let's bring him in. But we need to be careful. We don't want to spook him before we have enough evidence to make an arrest."

Morgan nodded in agreement. They had to be careful not to let Jim Alba slip through their fingers. She grabbed her coat and headed out the door, with Derik following close behind.

***

Morgan let Derik drive on the way to Grace Alba's house. As he cut through the dreary afternoon, Morgan sat in the passenger seat, listening to the windshield wipers swipe across the windshield. Her mind wandered, going over the details of the case, then lingering back into her time in prison, always hanging over her like a cloud.

Then, there was Derik. Working together again felt strange but right. Morgan had to admit that she still admired Derik Greene. He was always good-looking back in the day, but he'd aged well, with delicate crow's feet on his pale face around his blue eyes. She wasn't sure why she was noticing it now, but he looked good. Part of her had always wondered if the two of them would ever end up getting together, even as a fling, but it had never happened.

Then Morgan went to jail.

She sighed, pushing it aside, reminding herself it wasn't appropriate.

As they pulled up to the house, Morgan took a deep breath and steeled herself for the conversation ahead. It was a modest, ranch style house with white siding and a red, shingled roof. The front lawn was impeccably manicured, with a garden full of vibrant red roses and pale pink tulips. A white picket fence encompassed the back yard, and a pair of rocking chairs sat on the porch. Morgan could see the body she'd seen earlier—Grace—alive here, happy here. Then she saw the bruises on Grace's arms during the autopsy, and she wondered if life wasn't so perfect after all.

Still, she had to keep an open mind. They didn't know what type of man Jim Alba would be, not yet.

They got out of the car and breezed through the stormy afternoon. Morgan felt the light drizzle on her clothes before she took refuge under the awning of the porch.

Morgan knocked on the door. Moments later, they were greeted at the door by a tall, broad-shouldered man with dark hair and a solemn expression. Morgan recognized him from his file: Jim Alba. He didn't have much emotion on his face, barely even looked upset, considering his wife was murdered today.

"I'm Special Agent Morgan Cross with the FBI," Morgan said, showing her badge. "This is Special Agent Derik Greene. Are you Jim Alba?"

He nodded. "I'm assuming this is about my wife."

"We're sorry for your loss," Morgan said.

Jim nodded, then stepped aside to let them in. Morgan and Derik followed him into the living room, where they took a seat on the couch. By all accounts, it looked to be a charming home. The living room was a cheerful and inviting space with two comfortable couches in a sunny yellow hue, a modern coffee table with glossy black finish, and cream-colored walls dotted with bright, abstract art pieces. On the mantle was a photo of Grace, smiling, and Jim, smiling, too, but with more darkness in his eyes. Morgan eyed Jim up as he sat down on one of the couches, gesturing for Morgan and Derik to do the same. Morgan sat down on the stiff couch, breathing in the smell of the vanilla candle on the end table beside her.

"I'm sorry to bother you at home, Mr. Alba," Morgan said. "We just have a few questions about your wife, Grace, if you don't mind."

Jim nodded, his eyes darting nervously around the room. "Of course. Anything to help find who did this to her. I already told the police everything I know, but ..."

"It won't take long," Derik said.

Morgan noticed Jim's eyes flicker toward the door, as if he were thinking about making a run for it. She leaned forward, her eyes locked on his. "We just need to clear up some details, Mr. Alba. Can you tell us about your relationship with your wife?"

Jim cleared his throat. "We had our ups and downs like any marriage. But we were happy. I loved her."

"And did she ever mention if she was having any problems, or if anyone was bothering her?" Morgan asked.

Jim shook his head. "No, she didn't say anything like that. She was pretty private about those sorts of things."

Morgan leaned back, studying Jim's face. There was something off about him, but she couldn't quite put her finger on it. "Can you tell us where you were this morning?"

"I was here," he said. "I drove Milly to school. Grace was supposed to be at work, but obviously, that never happened."

"You don't seem very torn up about that," Derik pointed out. "Your wife has just been murdered, Mr. Alba."

Jim glanced around, but his expression remained dull. "I was raised in a household where showing emotion is considered a weakness. I have my own way of coping with this. I'm more concerned about my daughter."

"Where is your daughter?" Morgan asked.

"I dropped her off with her babysitter," Jim replied. "She doesn't know what's happened yet. I'm still getting everything prepared."

Convenient, Morgan thought. "Can anyone corroborate your whereabouts at the time Grace was murdered?" she asked.

Jim's eyes flashed. "Excuse me?"

"They're just standard questions," Derik intercepted.

"It sounds like you're accusing me of murdering my wife," Jim said plainly, and Morgan was taken aback by his calm, yet blunt nature.

She could work with this, though. She could be blunt too.

"Were you aware of the bruises your wife had at the time of her death?" Morgan asked. "They were far too old to have been done the same day she died."

"I know nothing about that," Jim snapped back. He stood up, his domineering aura seeping into the room like dark water. "And I think I'm going to have to ask you to leave."

Morgan stood, too, unwavering. "Is that because you're guilty, Mr. Alba?"

"We're just asking questions," Derik cut in, attempting to cool the tension, but it was too late for that.

Morgan stared down Jim, unafraid. She didn't trust this guy, not for a second.

"You can speak to me when I have a lawyer," Jim said. "Now, get out of my house."

Morgan nodded, keeping her gaze locked with Jim's as she slowly made her way toward the door. Derik followed behind her, tense and ready for anything. Just as they reached the threshold, Jim called out to them.

"You two may want to watch your backs," he said icily. "People who ask too many questions sometimes end up in trouble."

Morgan turned around, her eyes narrowing. "Is that a threat, Mr. Alba?" she asked.

Jim shrugged. "Take it as you will. I'm just an ordinary man who lost his wife."

He slammed the door behind them.

Morgan and Derik left the house, the tension palpable between them. It was bold, brazen, to threaten two FBI agents like that, as vague as it might be. There was something off about him, something that didn't quite add up. As they got back into the car, her thoughts turned to the bruises on Grace's arms. Were they a sign of domestic abuse or something else entirely? And what about Jim's strange behavior? He seemed too calm for someone who just lost his wife. The pieces of the puzzle were starting to come together, but there were still too many gaps.

"What was that all about?" Derik asked once they were inside the car.

"I don't know," Morgan replied, still thinking over the encounter. "But I don't trust him. Something about him just doesn't add up."

"I agree," Derik said. "But we need more evidence before we can make any accusations. He'll be bringing in a lawyer, so we better have a case."

"I think he's lying," Morgan said. "Did you notice how calm he was the whole time? And he didn't seem to care about his wife's death at all."

"I noticed," Derik replied. "But that doesn't necessarily mean he's guilty."

"I know," Morgan said. "But something about him just doesn't sit right with me."

"So, what now?"

Morgan stared out at Jim's house. Through the curtains, he peered out at them, glowering, before he pulled them shut. It was odd that his wife was dead, and the first thing he did was send his daughter away. It occurred to Morgan that even if Jim wouldn't talk—they could still get dirt on him and Grace's marriage.

And their child's babysitter could be just who they needed to talk to.

CHAPTER FIVE

The babysitter, a young woman named Lisa, lived in a small apartment complex on the other side of town. As they walked up to her door, Morgan felt a sense of unease. Something about the whole situation didn't sit right with her, and Jim's calm demeanor had left a bad taste in her mouth. She couldn't imagine how fun it had been for Grace to be married to a man who could be that cold. She wondered why Grace stayed, or why she'd fallen for him in the first place. There were so many things about her that Morgan—that no one—would ever understand about Grace Alba.

But the babysitter might be able to provide some window into the married couple's lives.

Lisa answered the door, looking surprised to see them. She was a perky young woman, no older than twenty, with blonde hair in a high ponytail.

Morgan and Derik flashed their badges, and Lisa's eyebrows went up.

"O-oh, my," Lisa said. "Is this about what happened to—" She cut herself off, glancing behind her into the apartment. Morgan could see Milly, the eight-year-old girl, watching cartoons on the couch. Right; Jim had mentioned that Milly didn't know yet.

"It's about Grace, yes," Morgan said. "Can we come in?"

Lisa hesitated before stepping aside to let them in. Milly looked over, and the innocent look on the girl's face broke Morgan's heart. It reminded her of when she got home from prison and saw her dog, Skunk, for the first time in years. His big, innocent eyes, that still knew her, had no idea of the hell she'd gone through.

"Milly, you stay here, okay?" Lisa said. "I'm going to talk to the nice people in my bedroom."

Milly nodded, happy to keep watching TV.

Lisa led them into a bedroom and closed the door. Morgan noticed that Lisa's hands were shaking.

"Is everything okay?" Derik asked.

Lisa took a deep breath. "I'm just a little nervous. I've never talked to the FBI before, and it's so awful what happened to Grace ... when Jim told me, I was beside myself, but I'm trying to keep it together for Milly's sake. She'll be devastated when she finally finds out."

"We understand," Morgan said, trying to put Lisa at ease. "Can you tell us about Jim and Grace's relationship? Did they have any issues?"

Lisa hesitated. "I don't know if I should be talking about this. It's not really my place."

"We're trying to piece together what happened to Grace," Derik said. "Anything you can tell us could be helpful."

Lisa bit her lip, thinking. "Well, they had their problems like any couple, I guess. Jim could be a little controlling—he wanted things done his way, you know? And Grace was always so sweet, she just went along with it. But sometimes, I could see it got to her. Like when Jim would snap at her or get angry over little things. Jim loved Grace, I'm sure of it. But sometimes ... I don't know, it was like he didn't appreciate her enough. Like he took her for granted."

"That's helpful," Derik said. "Did Grace ever talk to you about any problems in their marriage?"

Lisa shook her head. "No, not really. She was always very private." Lisa bit her lip, looking hesitant. "I don't know if I should be saying this, but they did argue sometimes. And I did notice some bruises on Grace's arms one time when she picked up Milly. I didn't say anything, but I was worried. She just brushed it off and said she had fallen down the stairs."

Morgan's heart sank. It seemed like the bruises were a sign of domestic abuse after all.

"And how was their relationship with Milly?" Derik asked.

"They loved her," Lisa said, her eyes tearing up. "They were amazing parents. But I always got the feeling that something was off between Jim and Grace. Like they were just going through the motions."

Morgan nodded, taking in Lisa's words. It sounded like there was more going on than Jim had let on. She wondered if Grace had confided in anyone else about the abuse, or if she had kept it all to herself. Either way, they needed more evidence if they were going to build a case against Jim.

"Did you ever witness any of the arguments between them?" Morgan asked.

Lisa shook her head. "No, they never fought in front of me. But sometimes I could hear them arguing behind closed doors. It was always about little things, like money or chores, but sometimes it would escalate into yelling."

Morgan and Derik exchanged a glance. There was certainly more happening behind closed doors with Grace and Jim's marriage.

"Thank you for your help, Lisa," Morgan said, handing her a card with their contact information. "If you think of anything else, please don't hesitate to call us."

Lisa nodded, apprehension on her face. Morgan hesitated to leave. It seemed like they'd gotten all of the information they could from Lisa, but at the same time, they still didn't have enough. They needed something more solid to build a true case against Jim. Lisa never saw any of the abuse, so it still wasn't confirmed.

An idea suddenly struck Morgan.

Grace wasn't the only victim, after all. There were three others, all who shared a physical resemblance with Grace. It may have been a shot in the dark, but Morgan took out her phone and opened a picture of the victims, starting with the first: Nelly Swanson.

"Have you ever seen this woman before?" Morgan asked.

Lisa observed the photo, then shook her head.

Morgan swiped to the next, victim number two: Patty Harris. Another red head in her thirties.

Once more, Lisa shook her head.

It was probably going nowhere, but Morgan had to try. She swiped to a photo of the third victim, Mia Jones.

At that one, Lisa's face changed. She bit her lip and observed it more.

"I did see her," Lisa said, and Morgan's pulse jumped. "She was at Jim and Grace's house the last time I babysat for them. She stood out because I thought she looked a lot like Grace, but I didn't know who she was or why she was there. I assumed a family friend."

"And when was this?" Derik asked.

"We need to know the exact day," Morgan clarified, her voice serious.

Lisa nodded. "It was Wednesday."

Morgan's stomach sank as she shared a look with Derik. The expression on his face told her all she needed to know.

They were on the same page.

Because Wednesday was also the day Mia died.

***

The first thing Morgan did when they left Lisa's apartment was call AD Mueller.

His stern voice came through the phone as the elevator reached the bottom floor. Morgan and Derik ran outside into the dreary afternoon.

"Cross, what's going on?" AD Mueller asked. "I've been up to my eyeballs in paperwork, but—"

"Sir, I need a team," Morgan said, phone pressed to her ear. She jogged after Derik through the parking lot, and they took refuge in the car, Derik behind the wheel. Morgan buckled up her seatbelt. "I'm gonna send you an address, okay?" Morgan said. "I need a team there now."

"Care to explain what this is about?" Mueller asked.

Morgan shared a look with Derik, who wore the same serious expression Morgan was sure she wore too. They didn't have time to waste. Jim Alba just might be the killer they were looking for, and they had to search his house.

"An eyewitness has placed Mia at Grace's house before they were both killed," Morgan explained. "It's credible, Mueller. The babysitter saw Mia at Grace's house, and we have strong reason to believe Jim Alba was physically abusive toward Grace. We need a team and a warrant by the time we get back to his house—should be ten minutes."

AD Mueller was quiet on the other end of the line, and Morgan held her breath as Derik kept driving. She was going in there, team or no team, but they needed that warrant.

After a moment, Mueller said, "You sound confident about this, Cross. I'm willing to take your word, and I can get that warrant expedited, hopefully within ten."

Morgan sighed in relief. "Thank you, sir. We'll be there soon."

She hung up and turned to Derik. "We need to hurry."

Derik nodded and pressed down hard on the gas pedal, the car speeding through the streets. Morgan's heart was racing in her chest. They were so close to finding out the truth. But at the same time, she felt a sense of dread. What if Jim had already fled? What if he had already gotten rid of any evidence? They'd tipped him off, she realized, by going in there without enough to bring him in.

But they could still catch him. Lisa's statement alone would be enough, and Morgan was sure whatever they found in the house would back it up even more.

As they drove, she thought about Jim and Grace Alba—a perfect couple on the outside, with something darker lying within. In all of this, she knew that their daughter, Milly, was a victim too; not only had she lost her mother, but there was a good chance she could lose her father too. Morgan felt for the little girl. It reminded her that once, long ago, before Morgan went to prison, she'd wanted a life of her own like theirs, without the darkness. A husband. A child. A home with a white picket fence.

That ship had sailed for her. She was forty, bitter, and had missed out on ten years of her life, and for what? A bad call gone wrong.

She glanced at Derik as he drove. She'd barely gotten the chance to get to know him again, as a person, after she got out. He'd told her he'd divorced, but she didn't know the details; if he ever dated again, if he had kids, if he even wanted them. A lot could happen in ten years, and a lot could change in a person's life.

Morgan realized that she didn't want to know.

Thinking about anything other than the case at hand was a distraction she couldn't afford. It was better not to get too close to anyone. Relationships only led to pain and heartbreak, as evidenced by Grace Alba's tragic end. Better to focus on the case and justice, she thought. That was what mattered now.

CHAPTER SIX

The car screeched to a halt in front of Jim Alba's house, and Morgan and Derik were out of the car in a flash, running toward the front door. FBI cars were already surrounding the house as well. Morgan banged hard on the door, her heart pounding in her chest. The rest of the team assembled behind them, and Morgan was grateful to know everything had worked out. Mueller had gotten the warrant, and now, it wasn't just her and Derik facing off against this guy. He had the full force of the FBI on him.

He wouldn't get away with what he'd done.

When there was no answer, she turned to Derik, who nodded in agreement. They kicked the door down and rushed in, guns drawn.

The house was eerily quiet. Morgan looked around for any sign of Jim but found nothing. What little warmth had existed in this house during their earlier visit was gone.

"He might still be here," Morgan said to the team behind her. "Let's search the house and find him."

The team split up, each taking a different room to search. Morgan and Derik began with the living room, searching for any clues as to where Jim might have gone. But the room was empty, save for a few pieces of furniture and family photos. Morgan's eyes lingered on a photo of Jim and Grace, both smiling at the camera with their arms around each other. It was impossible to tell from the photo that anything was wrong between them.

But Morgan knew better now. The evidence against Jim was mounting, and she was sure they would find something incriminating in this house.

"Let's check the kitchen," Derik said, gesturing toward the doorway.

They moved through the house, checking every room and closet, but there was no sign of Jim. Morgan's frustration grew with each empty room. Where was he?

As they reached the kitchen, Morgan's senses sharpened. Morgan's gaze darted around the kitchen, taking in every detail. Her eyes focused on the counters, the cupboards, and the floor, searching for any signs of disturbance or clues that might tell her where Jim had gone. She was alert and ready for anything, her body tensed, ready to respond at a moment's notice. Morgan noticed the faint glimmer of the metal countertops and the intricate patterns of tiles on the floor. She heard the subtle creaking of the floorboards and smelled a faint, musky scent in the air. Her vision sharpened; her focus narrowed in on every detail as she mentally prepared herself for whatever was ahead.

On the kitchen tables, there were several ads for contractors and gardeners. Morgan looked out back, noting that the garden was well-kept, even though it seemed neither Grace nor Jim had a history of being interested in the hobby, according to their files and financial records.

Then she saw it: the basement door was ajar. She nodded at Derik, and he nodded back.

They descended the stairs cautiously, guns still drawn. The basement was dimly lit, with a musty smell that made Morgan's nose wrinkle in disgust. The concrete walls were lined with shelves, filled with tools and various knick-knacks. Morgan's eyes roamed the room, looking for any signs of Jim.

The musty smell grew stronger, and she could hear a faint humming sound coming from the depths of the basement. She saw a small flicker of light coming from the back corner of the room.

She quickly made her way toward the source of the light, her heart pounding in her chest. As she got closer, she could hear Jim's voice, mumbling to himself. She peered around the corner, her gun pointed directly at him.

Jim was sitting in front of a computer, feverishly typing away. He looked up as Morgan entered the room, a look of shock and fear crossing his face. He stood up abruptly.

"What the—"

"Jim Alba, you're under arrest," Morgan said, keeping her gun pointed at him. "We have a warrant to search this house."

"How did you get in here!?" It seemed he hadn't even noticed or heard them come in, he was too caught up in whatever it was that he was doing on his computer.

"What do we have here?" Derik asked, stepping up. Jim kept his eyes trained on Morgan—and her gun—but she peered past him, too, at the computer screen. It looked like an email. Morgan couldn't read it from far away, but Derik got closer and said out loud, "Wow, explains why you're not so torn up about Grace's death."

"What?" Morgan said.

Jim had sweat on his brow, his eyes wide and crazed.

"He's having an affair," Derik said. "It's obvious right here. 'I need to come see you, baby. They're going to go after me for Grace. I can just leave Milly.'"

Disgust curled in Morgan's stomach as she looked back at Jim. He was worse than she could ever have imagined.

"You're a real piece of work, Jim," Morgan said, disgust lacing her words. "You're a liar and a cheater, and now you're a murderer too."

"I'm not a murderer," he said. "I didn't do it."

Just then, they heard the sound of feet thumping down the stairs. Two of the men from the team appeared beside Morgan and Derek. Morgan gestured for the team to apprehend him. "Take him away."

"This is bullshit," Jim shouted. "I didn't kill my wife!"

"Yeah, we'll see about that," Morgan muttered, more to Derik than anyone else. He silently nodded beside her.

As Jim was led out of the basement in handcuffs, Morgan couldn't help but feel a twinge of satisfaction. They had caught the man who had killed Grace and left her daughter motherless. Justice would be served.

Morgan took a glance at the emails, still open on the computer screen. There were dozens of them, all detailing Jim's affair with a woman named "Amelia." It seemed like he'd killed Grace for a reason—to get rid of her—but it made Morgan curious. Why kill the other three women before her if his end goal was to just get her out of the way so he could pursue his affair?

They went back upstairs, and as they did, Morgan spotted a car out front of the house. She frowned and watched through the window, and that was when she realized that it was Lisa and Milly.

Milly ran out of the car, followed by Lisa. Morgan stormed outside as light rain sprinkled down on them. Jim was being shoved into the back of a car.

"Daddy!" Milly called out.

A desperate looking Lisa grabbed Milly's arm. Morgan stormed over to them. "Why did you bring her here?" Morgan called out.

"She saw her mom on the news," Lisa stammered. "I-I didn't know what else to do. I thought Jim would be gone by now, and she was crying and begging to go home."

Morgan's eyes met with Milly's. The little girl looked small and lost; her eyes filled with tears as she watched her father being taken away. Morgan's heart ached for her. She knew the pain of losing a parent all too well.

She walked over to Milly, crouching down in front of her. "Hey," she said softly, "I know this is really hard, but it's going to be okay. You're safe now."

Milly looked up at her with wide, teary eyes. "But what about me? What's going to happen to me now? Where is my dad going? And where is my mom? The news said she was ..."

Morgan's heart broke at the raw pain and confusion in the little girl's voice. She put a comforting hand on Milly's shoulder, trying to find the right words to say. But she realized then that she wasn't a comforting or maternal person at all. Milly shrugged away from her touch, and Morgan dropped her hand. She didn't have any words at all.

She looked up at Lisa, who wrapped an arm around Milly's shoulder.

"You're going to stay with me, Milly," Lisa said, "until your dad can take you home, okay?"

Morgan stood up and watched as Lisa ushered Milly back to the car. She knew that it wasn't going to be easy for the little girl, but she couldn't help but feel that she had let her down in some way. She watched the car drive away, her mind racing with all the questions that still needed answers. She had caught Jim, but that didn't explain why he had killed all those women before his wife. She needed more evidence, but where was she going to find it?

She took one last look at the house, trying to piece together everything that had happened there. It was a house full of secrets, of lies, and of pain. She couldn't shake the feeling that there was more to the story than what she had uncovered so far. She needed to find out what had really happened to all those women, and why Jim had felt he needed to kill them. She had a feeling that the answers were hiding somewhere in that house, waiting to be uncovered.

Morgan turned to Derik, who was watching her with a concerned look on his face. "What's our next move?" he asked.

Morgan shook her head, feeling lost and unsure. "I don't know," she admitted. "We need to keep investigating, find out what Jim's motive was for killing." She couldn't help but feel a lick of bitterness. "I just don't get it. That man had everything. Why'd he throw it all away?"

In another life, Morgan would have killed for a lovely little girl like Milly, for a house like this. Of course, she didn't say that to Derik. He never knew that she'd dreamed of starting a family one day.

But that dream had died long ago, buried beneath the weight of her job, the trauma she had faced, and the scars that marked her past. Still, something about this case had struck a chord with her, had made her feel like she was fighting for something more than just justice. She wondered if the little girl would ever be able to understand the horrors that had happened in her own home, the crimes that her father had committed. She wondered if she would ever be able to move past it, to heal and grow up without the weight of that knowledge dragging her down. She wondered if justice would ever truly be served for Grace and the other women who had lost their lives because of Jim's actions.

There were no easy answers, no quick fixes. And for Morgan, there would be no fairy tale endings either. She'd lost her father while she was wrongfully in prison. She'd missed out on most of her dog's life. And now, she was forty years old, and if she did decide to have a child, it might be harder on her than it would've been before. Going to prison had stolen so much from her, and the weight of that hit her in full force, like a tidal wave swallowing her whole.

Derik looked at her, concern etched on his face. "Are you okay?" he asked.

She wasn't okay, but she had to keep it in check. "Let's just go question this guy."

***

Morgan sat across from Jim Alba in the interrogation room, letting Derik take the lead, because Jim had turned into a closed book. Morgan was too angry, too rattled, to ask questions with an even head. She had found herself feeling extremely frustrated toward Jim, this man who had everything, who may have just thrown it all away, and for what?

His daughter would suffer because of it too.

The man was completely selfish.

“Mr. Alba, please,” Derik said, playing up the nice cop act, “the sooner you talk to us, the sooner we can work on getting you out of here.”

Jim glanced at Morgan. “Bullshit. You aren’t letting me go. I can tell by the way that one’s looking at me.”

Morgan couldn’t help but laugh. Derik sighed, meeting Jim’s eyes. “I need you to tell me about your relationship with your wife. You were clearly having an affair.”

Jim's face twisted into a scowl as he leaned back in his chair. "She wasn't just my mistress, if that's what you're asking," he spat. "She was the love of my life. Grace was nothing but a burden."

Morgan's blood boiled at the mention of Grace. She knew that Jim was lying, that he was just trying to deflect from the truth. She leaned forward, her voice cold and steady. "You killed Grace, didn't you?"

Jim's eyes widened in surprise, but he quickly composed himself. "I don't know what you're talking about."

Morgan leaned in even closer, her voice lowering to a dangerous growl. "Lying won't help you here. We have you, Jim. We know."

"You have no idea what you're talking about," Jim said, "and you’re wasting time on the wrong guy. I didn't kill my wife."

Morgan leaned back in her chair, studying Jim. She wasn't buying it. There was something in his eyes, a flicker of fear, that made her believe he had something to do with Grace's death.

"Then who did?" Derik asked, his voice firm. "Because we have evidence that points to you."

Jim scoffed, shaking his head. "I don't know." Jim shifted in his seat, avoiding Morgan's gaze. "Look, I loved Grace. But she was ... difficult. She didn't understand me the way that Maria did. And when she found out about us ..." he trailed off, his voice barely above a whisper.

"When she found out about your affair, she threatened to leave you," Morgan finished for him. "Is that when you decided to kill her?"

Jim's eyes flicked up to hers, then back down to the table. "I didn't kill her," he repeated. "I swear, I didn't. And I don't want to talk to you anymore without a lawyer present."

Morgan tensed up, and Derik let out a sigh. That wasn't good. If they had to wait on Jim's lawyer, it could delay their interrogation way longer than Morgan had hoped.

"Are you sure about that?" Morgan asked.

"I'm pretty damn sure," Jim shot back.

Derik stood up, nodding. "Okay, Jim. Until your lawyer can arrive, you're going to be staying here, with us. We'll have someone come in and process you."

Morgan left the room with Derik, feeling a sense of disappointment wash over her. She had been so close to getting a confession out of him, but he had remained stubborn, denying any involvement in Grace's death. It was frustrating, to say the least, but Morgan wasn't one to give up easily. She knew that there had to be more to the story, more evidence to uncover, in order to truly bring Jim to justice.

And it was late now. Chances were, the lawyer wouldn't come until the morning, which left them spinning their wheels until then. As she walked down the hall with Derik, she felt like the walls were closing in on her. All those thoughts she'd had earlier, about how much of her life she'd missed, came flooding back, filling her with panic. It didn't seem fair that people like Jim Alba could live in the world and get what they want, while she was locked away for so long when she was completely innocent.

"Cross, you sure you're okay?" Derik asked.

"No, I'm not okay," she snapped, turning away as the darkening sky growled above, and more rain fell on them.

"Cross—"

"No!" Morgan snapped, emotion hitting her like a whip. She could admit that part of her did resent Derik. "Why did you stop fighting for me?"

"What?" Confusion flickered all over his face.

"When I went to jail," Morgan said, knowing she was being out of line, but unable to stop it. "I know it wasn't your job, but—we were friends. No, we were more than friends." She wasn't even talking about the stupid kiss they'd shared. She didn't even want to bring that up. But they had been partners, above all else.

Derik looked taken aback by Morgan's outburst. "You know I did everything I could," he said softly. "But the evidence was stacked against you, and there was only so much I could do. I told you, I'm sorry for giving up."

Morgan turned to face him, her eyes filled with anger and hurt. "That's not good enough," she said. "You were supposed to be my friend, my partner. You were supposed to fight for me, no matter what."

"I did fight for you," Derik insisted. "But sometimes, the system just isn't fair. You of all people should know that. As the years went on, I went through my own shit, and I just … I didn't know what else to do for you."

Morgan shook her head, feeling a rage building inside her. It wasn't at Derik anymore, but at the world. She felt bad for exploding on him, that he was in her line of fire, but she couldn't help it. "You don't get it," she said. "You don't know what it's like to be behind bars, to be treated like a criminal when you know you're innocent. You don't know what it's like to lose everything you ever cared about."

"Morgan, I—"

"No," she cut him off. She didn't want to hear it. She just wanted to be alone.

Without another thought, Morgan took off. She needed to clear her head.

CHAPTER SEVEN

Back at home, Morgan buried herself in case files to distract herself from her earlier embarrassment. She shouldn't have snapped at Derik like that. It was unfounded and unprofessional. But something about the whole situation had made her snap.

She sighed, leaning back on her couch. Her table lamp was on, filling the living room with a soft, warm glow. Beside her, Skunk wagged his tail and looked up at her with milky eyes. When Morgan had first got the Pitbull, before she went to prison, he'd been just a puppy. She hoped Derik could understand why she'd snapped, how hard it was for her to have gone to jail at thirty and been released at forty, ten years later. She was more muscular, hardened, jaded, but deep inside, she was still her. The more time she spent out of prison, the more she remembered that.

But the memories also brought back the pain, the trauma, the fear. The fear of being locked up again, of being accused of a crime she didn't commit. She couldn't afford to make any more mistakes, any more missteps. She needed to stay focused, to keep digging until she found the answers she was looking for.

Skunk whined and nosed at her hand, and Morgan absently petted his head. It was getting late—night had settled over the town, and Jim Alba was being detained for the night. They'd question him properly tomorrow, once he had his lawyer secured, but Morgan was just grateful they'd caught the bastard, and he was behind bars, which meant more women were safe. Still, she needed to build as strong of a case against him as she could.

She just hoped Jim Alba was the right guy. Either way, he was the best lead they had.

Try as she might, her mind kept going back to Derik's face when she'd snapped earlier, and her face burned with embarrassment. She needed a break from the case, from the memories that threatened to overwhelm her. She needed to clear her head.

She grabbed her keys and put on her coat, Skunk following closely behind her. As she threw on her jacket, she knelt down and rubbed her dog's head. "I'll be back soon, boy. Just need to get out of here for a bit."

Skunk whined but then went over to his bed like a good boy. Morgan smiled before she headed out into the night.

The sky had cleared, revealing the stars above. She walked to the nearest bar, a dive that she used to frequent before her arrest. She pushed open the door and stepped inside, the familiar scent of alcohol and smoke greeting her. She felt a pang of nostalgia, of regret, as she walked up to the bar.

The bartender was the same as he'd always been, just older. Gareth, now in his fifties, was just as spry as he'd always been as he poured two beers on tap for a couple and handed it off to them, just as Morgan slid into the barstool. When Gareth noticed her, he looked like he'd seen a ghost.

"Hey, Gareth," Morgan said.

"Well, shit," Gareth said. "Morgan Cross, is that you? I thought you'd gone and moved away."

"I did, sort of," Morgan said, grateful that her fate hadn't exactly spread to the bar. Some of the neighbors knew, but ten years was a long time to go away. She was sure most people in general had forgotten about her.

Gareth raised an eyebrow. "Sort of?" he asked.

"I was in prison for ten years," Morgan said, and Gareth's eyes widened in shock. "But I'm out now. Trying to get my life back on track."

A flicker of recognition on Gareth's face. "I thought I heard someone talking about some FBI agent who was wrongfully convicted. That you?"

Sullenly, Morgan nodded.

Gareth shook his head, sympathy written all over his face. "I had no idea, Morgan. I'm sorry."

Morgan shrugged, trying to play it off. "It's in the past now. Just trying to move forward, you know?"

Gareth nodded, then gestured to the beer he'd poured for her. "On the house," he said.

Morgan gave him a small smile. "Thanks, Gareth."

As she sipped her beer, she looked around the bar. It was a Monday night, and the place was mostly empty. There were a few regulars scattered around, nursing their drinks and watching the TV screen playing in the corner. Morgan felt a sense of belonging, of familiarity, that she hadn't felt in a long time. Maybe it was the alcohol, or maybe it was the company, but for the first time in a while, she felt like she was home.

Morgan took it all in, the sights and sounds of the bar, the way the bartender moved with ease. It was a reminder of a past life, of a time before prison, before everything had gone to shit. She missed it—the carefree days of drinking with friends, of not worrying about anything but having a good time when it was off-hours and taking down criminals when she was working.

But those days were gone, and she couldn't dwell on them. She took a deep breath and downed the rest of her beer, feeling the slight buzz in her head. The more she drank, the more Derik slipped back into her mind.

She hated how they'd left things off. Tomorrow, they were back at work. She had to make it right. Maybe call him, tell him she was sorry. No—that wouldn't be enough. She'd known Derik Greene for too long, even if they'd been apart for ten years.

Maybe it was a bad idea, but at that moment, she decided what she'd do.

***

Morgan knocked on Derik's door, having taken a cab across the city. The lights were on inside, telling her he was home. This place was new—different from the apartment he'd lived at the last time she'd been at one of his places. It was a small, modest house, with dark blue paneling in a family neighborhood. She wondered if she was about to get greeted by his wife or girlfriend—or worse, a kid—but when the door opened, it was just Derik on the other side. His plaid pajamas and ruffled dark hair made him look younger than he was, more like how he used to look to her.

"Morgan?" His blue eyes widened in shock.

"Hey." With a tight-lipped smile, she held up the bottle of scotch she'd grabbed on the way over. "Apology drink?"

He rubbed the back of his neck. "I don't know, Cross. It's late. We need to work."

"It'll only take a bit."

Hesitantly, Derik stepped aside. Morgan breezed into his home and was surprised by how messy the place was, giving off the instant vibe of a bachelor pad. She noticed the diet soda cans piling up on the kitchen counter through the entrance, along with the stack of dishes. And there were a few hoodies lying around the living room, something she was sure a live-in girlfriend would never allow. In a way, it reminded her of her own place, minus Skunk.

Derik followed her, his frown deepening as she made herself at home on his couch. Derik set down a cup.

"Where's yours?" Morgan asked.

"None for me," he said. "I've been sober since the divorce."

She never remembered Derik having a drinking problem, but then again, ten years was a long time.

"I'm sorry about earlier," Morgan said. Derik sat down a full couch cushion away, still looking unsure. "I shouldn't have snapped at you like that. It's just been a long day, and I needed to blow off some steam."

Derik shrugged. "It's fine, Morgan. I get it. This case is getting to all of us."

Morgan shook her head. "No, it's not just that. I've been thinking a lot about the past. About how much I've lost." She looked away. "And about us."

Derik's eyebrows shot up. "Us? Morgan, we haven't been partners in ten years. Still, it hurt when you said I didn't fight for you."

"I know, I know," Morgan said, running her fingers through her hair. "But I just ... I don't know. Working with you today, then seeing how Jim Alba had such a perfect life, thrown away all for nothing ... it brought back a lot of memories. It reminded me of things I used to dream about."

Derik looked down at his hands. "You never told me what you dreamt about. You were always a closed book."

Her eyes flashed to his. "Well, I've been locked up for a long time. Maybe I'm sick of being a closed book."

"So, what am I supposed to say?" Derik said. "I did fight for you, Morgan. Maybe I could've tried harder, but things got complicated in my life too."

Morgan sipped the scotch, enjoying the warmth in her throat. She wished Derik would have a drink with her like he used to, but if he'd made an effort to stay sober, she had to respect that. She realized then that she never did get caught up on his life.

"What happened with you?" she asked him.

He laughed. "That's a big topic."

Morgan took another sip. "I've got time."

Derik sighed, leaning back in the couch, and Morgan found herself wishing he was just a bit closer to her. Maybe it was just the alcohol talking, but she was finding herself drawn to him.

"Things just got … so messy between us."

Morgan held her breath. She hoped it had nothing to do with that kiss they'd shared all those years ago …

"It just wasn't working out," Derik said. "As you know, things had been rocky for a long time."

She remembered. They never would've kissed like that if things with his wife had been perfect. She remembered them talking about taking a break before, which was part of how she'd justified the kiss back then, but looking back, it was wrong, no matter what. He'd still been married.

It was hard to picture Derik's married life after she went to jail. The thought that he'd had one, even if the marriage ended up failing, still made her envious. She never got to have a wedding. A chance to fall in love again. Not while she was locked up.

"I'm sorry," she said.

"Don't worry about it," Derik said, a small smile on his face. "I'm happy now. I've found a good balance in my life. Work, friends, and the occasional date."

Morgan shifted closer to him, feeling the heat of his body. "And what about love?" she asked. "Have you found that too?"

Derik's eyes met hers, and for a moment, Morgan thought she saw a flicker of something there. Something that made her heart race. But then he looked away, and the moment was gone.

"Not yet," he said softly. "But I'm not looking for it, either."

Morgan felt a pang of disappointment. She wondered if she'd read too much into that moment, or if she was just imagining things. But then she remembered something she'd read in a book once in her time in prison. She'd read a lot there. Something about how life was too short to not take risks. Too short to not go after what you wanted.

But then Derik said, "After everything that happened with Emma, I'm pretty turned off of love and family and all that crap. The idea used to matter to me. I used to want kids, I used to dream about my perfect life with my perfect family. But I thought I had it, then it died in the worst way possible."

Morgan's heart sank. "What happened?"

"She cheated on me," Derik said. "A full-blown affair that had been going on for at least a year. We divorced right after I found out."

"Damn," Morgan said. She felt for Derik. Even with their heat-of-the-moment kiss, they had never engaged in an actual affair. Both were bad, she knew that, but what Emma had done was certainly worse. "Sorry," she added.

"Yeah, well, it's all good," Derik said. "I started drinking too much after that, but then I turned my life around and got sober. Still, I've pretty much accepted that I'm gonna die alone. Love's not for everyone." He eyed the bottle of scotch but said nothing more.

"It's not too late for you," Morgan said, eyes lingering on his face. Derik always gave off the impression that he didn't know he was a handsome guy, but he was.

He looked at her, his eyes flicking up and down her face, stopping right at her lips.

Morgan felt her heart skip a beat. The tension between them was growing, and she couldn't deny the feelings that were stirring inside of her. She wanted Derik. Part of her had always wanted him.

Without thinking, Morgan leaned in and pressed her lips to Derik's. At first, he was still, his body tense under hers. But then, he relaxed and deepened the kiss, his hands finding their way to her waist. Morgan moaned softly into his mouth, running her fingers through his hair.

Then, in one quick motion, he pushed her away.

Morgan jolted back, smacked by the cold sting of rejection. Derik looked at her in shock, and embarrassment coursed through her. Morgan didn't think. She just stood up, grabbing the bottle of scotch as she did.

"Shit, sorry, Greene," she muttered.

She stumbled toward the door, scotch in hand, wondering how she could ever face Derik as her partner again.

She'd just royally messed everything up.

CHAPTER EIGHT

Morgan woke up too early the next day, before the sun was even up.

She took in the dismal landscape of the neighborhood as she walked, Skunk's paws padding the damp sidewalk beside her. Small, rundown houses lined the street, and many of them had boards nailed over their windows, giving them a depressing and eerie look. She could feel the alcohol from last night still buzzing in her veins and making her feel slightly warm, but the phone call she'd received in the early hours of the morning, plus her short hours of sleep, had sobered her right up. The street was empty, and a cold breeze blew, carrying with it the faint smell of garbage and smoke. The dark sky felt oppressive, casting a deep blanket of darkness over the street.

Up ahead, there was a man in a black hoodie. Just who she needed to see.

After Morgan had last talked to Samson, he'd floated the idea that Sandra Berryhill—his last victim—had a husband who was out of town, and that husband may have been the person who was there the night Morgan was framed for murder, for being Samson's accomplice.

But soon after, with some digging, Morgan found out that the husband truly *was* out of town. He was innocent. She'd confirmed it with ten-year-old footage of the man's trip, and he was in Canada at the time.

That left Morgan more confused, more lost, and so she'd gone back to Samson, played into his little game. He'd been so amused to see her again, to know he'd caught her attention. She'd asked him again who was there that night.

She'd hated herself for it, but she needed to know who framed her.

She needed to know why she'd lost ten years of her life.

He told her that he didn't know the man's name, but that he had an associate who could give her a name.

And now, here she was.

Skunk growled at the sight of him, but Morgan said, "It's okay, boy," and he calmed down. But the stranger looked at the dog, pausing for a moment. "He won't bite unless I tell him to," Morgan called out.

The man kept coming toward her. He stepped into the light of a streetlamp, revealing the gaunt face of a twenty-something man.

"You're Morgan Cross?" he asked.

"Yeah," she said. "Thanks for calling me back."

"Well, you have friends in high places," he said. "I've got the name you're looking for."

Morgan's heart picked up.

"Eric Domino," the stranger said. "That's the guy you're looking for."

Morgan gritted her teeth. She'd never heard of this Domino guy. But according to Samson, The Seven Signs Killer, another person had been on the scene the night Morgan had been framed. This person had stepped aside, allowing Samson to kill, and allowing Morgan to be framed for it. It had all ended in her ultimate arrest and ten years of her life gone, all for a misunderstanding. If that Domino guy had been there, he hadn't made it known. He'd disappeared.

"You're sure?" Morgan asked.

"I'm sure," he said. "He lives in an apartment building somewhere around here. That's all I can tell you."

Morgan nodded, feeling a sense of relief. She had a name now. It was a start.

"Thank you," she said to the stranger, then turned to leave. Skunk followed her, trotting by her side.

As she walked, Morgan couldn't help but feel a sense of unease. If Eric Domino was the missing piece to her story, then why had he disappeared? And why was he never mentioned in any of the reports or investigations? It seemed odd. There was so much more to this story—to *her* story—than she knew, and it infuriated her.

She needed to know why they did it.

And she needed to know *who* it was, so she could handle it accordingly.

What does that mean? she asked herself, even though she wasn't sure. Was she going to kill them? She couldn't do that—she wasn't a cold-blooded killer, even if she did want that person to pay. She could try to lock them up based on her word against theirs; after all, much of the media had grown to take Morgan's side, but she knew for a fact that there were still people out there who thought she belonged behind bars.

She found her car, parked on the side of the street, and opened the back door to let Skunk hop in. Then Morgan got behind the wheel and pulled out her laptop, opening it, and connecting to the FBI database. She looked right into one Eric Domino.

No match came up.

But Morgan wasn't convinced. She continued to dig deeper, looking for any clue as to why Domino had vanished that night. She pulled up old reports, witness statements, and anything she could find that was related to the case. As she delved deeper, she began to realize that there was something very wrong with the story of the Seven Signs Killer. And Eric Domino? He didn't seem to exist.

Was it a fake name? Or was the source lying to her?

There were too many unanswered questions, too many loose ends. And her gut was telling her that Eric Domino was the key to unlocking the truth. But how was she going to find him? There were many apartment buildings around here. Morgan supposed she could start at one and work her way through them.

Still, Morgan knew that she had to play this smart. She couldn't just show up at his doorstep and demand answers. She needed a plan, a way to get close to him and gain his trust. Or maybe doing it the old-fashioned way—with intimidation—could work better. Skunk was a good ally, after all ...

He barked happily as she glanced back at him, and she smiled. At the very least, she could go check out some of the buildings, see where he was living, get eyes on him.

She turned the keys in the ignition, her headlights cutting into the darkness of the unkempt street, ready to take off, just as her phone started ringing. It was nearly six a.m.—who would be calling her now?

She answered it, and her stomach sank.

Derik.

Morgan's hands shook as she answered the phone. "Derik?"

"Hey, Morgan." He sounded exhausted. "Glad you're up."

She couldn't take the anxiety. "I'm sorry about last night," she said.

"I'm not calling about that," Derik said. "I wanted you to come in early, so we can head to Mia Jones's house together. We know Mia was seen at Grace's house, so there might be some evidence at her house too. The police still have her place blocked off, so we can go in any time."

Morgan's stomach twisted with nerves. All Derik wanted to talk about was work. She didn't blame him.

"Sure, Greene," she said, trying to keep things professional. "Let's do that."

"Good. See you soon."

He hung up before she could get another word in.

Morgan sighed, looking back at Skunk. This was going to be a long day.

Quickly, Morgan checked the GPS on her phone. Mia Jones's address wasn't far from here—it was before Morgan's house, where she needed to drop Skunk off anyway. She could make a quick pitstop and get that over with, so she and Derik could work on other things first. Part of her knew better and knew she should run it by him, but in all honesty, she was dreading facing him. Maybe it was better to just do it alone.

Skunk whined from the back seat, sensing Morgan's tension. She reached back and patted his head. "Don't worry, boy. We'll get through this."

Morgan made a snap decision and put the car in drive. She would swing by Mia Jones's house and check it out real quick, then drop Skunk off and head into work. She couldn't help but feel like she was running away from her problems, but she didn't know how else to deal with them right now.

As she pulled up to Mia's house, she saw that it was still surrounded by police tape. She parked and got out, leaving Skunk in the car. She didn't want to risk him getting caught up in any evidence or police investigation.

Morgan slipped under the tape and started to examine the area. It was eerily quiet, and the only sounds were the chirping of crickets and the hum of distant traffic. The neighbors must have still been sleeping. Morgan walked toward the front door of the house, and she could already see signs of forced entry, likely from when the police had gone in. The door was slightly ajar, and she could see a darkened interior through the crack.

Morgan reached for her gun, feeling the familiar weight in her hand, just in case any squatters had made their way in during the investigation. Eyes were off Mia's house now, but it was still here. She stepped gingerly through the door, her eyes scanning the room for any signs of movement. There was nothing. It was just the shell of Mia Jones's life.

She wondered what had brought Mia to Grace and Jim's that day, how she even knew them. Maybe her affiliation to them was what got her killed, assuming Jim was the one who had done it. It was possible they were just friends, she supposed; they didn't live far from each other, and stranger things had happened.

It all made her sick, and Morgan made her way to the back yard. Like at Grace and Jim's, Mia's garden was pristine. Morgan stepped into the back yard as the sun began to rise, casting a cool blue hue as the sky slowly lightened.

She took a closer look at the garden. On the surface, it seemed completely normal. But then she looked closer. There was a smell in the air, like freshly cut grass. Mia had died days ago, and the police had taken over her house, and yet the work on this garden looked fresh.

She took a closer look at one of the leaves, then ran her finger along it.

A fresh cut.

Morgan's heart began to race as she realized what this meant. Someone had been here, tending to the garden, after Mia's death. But who? And why? Morgan's heart started to race. This was a significant detail, one that could lead to something. Someone had been tending to this garden recently, and it wasn't Mia. She looked around, trying to find any other signs of activity, but nothing seemed out of the ordinary.

She made her way back into the house, her mind racing with possibilities. There had to be a reason why someone was tending to Mia's garden. Maybe it was the killer, and he'd returned to the scene of one of his victims. He did seem to have an obsession with nature, after all—the mazes, for one, and the way he "planted" the bodies in the ground as if they were flowers. Maybe it was routine for him to revisit the homes of his dead, to trim their gardens as if they were still coming back to them, his own twisted way of paying homage.

Maybe he was even still in the neighborhood.

The thought filled her stomach with dread, and Morgan hurried through the house and back to her car, where Skunk was waiting for her.

If she was right, and the killer did do this, then there was no way Jim Alba was their killer.

They might have the wrong guy.
Which meant another woman's life could still be in danger.

CHAPTER NINE

He pressed his finger to the doorbell, and moments later, a lovely young woman answered the door. She was short—no taller than five feet—and curvy, with long, red hair and freckles splattered all over her cheeks.

She looked even better up close than she did from far away.

With his overalls on, his tools in his hands, he offered her a friendly smile. She looked up at him, confused, as she said, "Can I help you?"

"Yes," he said, "I'm here to make some adjustments to your garden."

"Oh?" Her brows pinched, confused. "I didn't ask for that ... we normally have Jerry come, and I think our next appointment is tomorrow."

"Jerry sent me," he clarified. "He's off this week, so I'm covering his clients. Guess I'm a bit ahead of schedule." He smiled wider, hoping she would accept it and invite him in.

She would, of course. He'd been watching her for weeks. He knew when she was home, when she was alone, and he knew how friendly she could be to her neighbors and people passing by. She was trusting, foolishly so.

As she stepped aside to let him in, he couldn't help but notice the way her hips swayed as she walked. He followed her into the living room, admiring the decor and the way the sunlight streamed through the windows, illuminating her curves.

As they passed by the kitchen, a voice on the radio flowed into the room:

"In other news, the Maze Killer is still at large, and police are not reporting that the FBI has taken over the case ..."

He smiled to himself. The FBI. They couldn't outsmart him, but they were worthy adversaries. He'd enjoy evading them, tricking them, over and over again.

"Isn't it just awful?" the girl said, looking back at him with those big eyes. "That Maze Killer, I mean ..."

"Oh, yes," he said. "Just terrible."

He suppressed a chuckle as she walked ahead, leading him to the back yard. She had no idea that the Maze Killer was standing right in front of her. She had no idea that he was the one responsible for the disappearances, for the fear that gripped the city. But she would soon learn, and she would learn the hard way.

He set down his tools and got to work, pretending to prune the flowers and trim the hedges. But his mind was far from the task at hand. He was already planning his next move, his next victim. He couldn't wait to see the fear in their eyes, the panic in their voices as they realized that they were trapped in his maze.

As the girl watched him work, he couldn't help but admire her beauty. He wondered what it would feel like to touch her, to taste her, to hear her scream his name. But he knew that he had to be patient. He couldn't risk getting caught, not now, not when he was so close to achieving his goal.

He trimmed the hedges as he was supposed to do. In truth, he liked this part of the façade, so sometimes he'd milk it, let it go on for longer than it needed to. Let the girl truly feel comfortable before she'd know the truth.

"Well, I'll let you finish up," she said, turning toward the back door.

In the morning light, her red hair was aflame. The sight of it, glimmering like fire, made his skin suddenly burn. Not with desire—with anger.

That hair. It was so bold. So vulgar. It had no business being natural, a color that vibrant.

Maybe it was time for her to learn already.

He slowly stood up, pulling a heavy tool from his belt, as she walked in the house through the back door, safely away from any chance of the neighbors seeing her.

He followed her, the tool heavy in his hand. He was careful to keep his footsteps silen as he crept behind her. He watched her walk toward the kitchen, humming to herself, not bothering to check behind her.

He raised the tool above his head, ready to strike. And then she turned around, and her eyes widened in terror when she saw him.

Before she could scream, he brought the tool down hard on her skull. There was a sickening thud as it made contact and then she crumpled to the ground, her red hair now matted with blood.

The Maze Killer stood over her, panting heavily, his pulse pounding in his ears. It was always the same rush, the same thrill, every time he took a life. He felt alive, powerful, invincible.

Now, for the fun part.

CHAPTER TEN

Morgan stormed into the FBI headquarters and headed toward the briefing room, only for Derik to appear right in front of her, his expression nothing short of angry. And Morgan was sure it wasn't about the kiss last night.

"What the hell, Cross?" Derik said. "I called you an hour ago, where were you?"

She pushed past him, continuing toward the briefing room, so they could talk in private, not in the public hall. She pushed inside, grateful for the quiet in the room. She faced Derik, ready to explain herself.

"Look, Mia's place was on my way," she said. "I stopped in myself."

"What?" Derik frowned. "We're supposed to be partners, Cross. We do things together. Why didn't you let me know?"

"Does it matter?" Morgan brushed off. "Look, I think we might be looking for a gardener or something. Mia's hedges were freshly trimmed. The killer could've returned and—"

"We agreed we wouldn't go off and do things without consulting the other," Derik interjected. "That was part of my conditions for being partners again."

"Conditions?" Morgan couldn't help the flame of offense that burned her. He was making her sound like a charity case, like he was doing her a favor by being partners with her again. "I'm not a charity case, Greene. I can work just fine on my own if you don't want to be my damn partner." She hadn't known Derik had set any "conditions" to working with her again, but now she was imagining him talking to Irvin the same way she did, only he was setting "rules" for how he'd handle Morgan, as if she needed to be handled with kid gloves.

Derik's eyes darkened at her response, his jaw clenching in anger. "That's not what I meant," he said through gritted teeth. "I just want us to work together as a team. That's how we'll catch this guy. But if you're gonna go off and do things on your own, then there's no point in us even being together."

"What the hell is your problem?" Morgan fired back.

"Right now, you are," Derik said. "You're out of line, Cross. With everything."

Morgan's stomach sank as she digested Derik's words. She could tell, now, this was about more than the case. It was also about her showing up at his house with a bottle of scotch and presumptuously kissing him.

She felt her cheeks flush with embarrassment. She had other things to worry about, like catching the Maze Killer. On top of that, Irvin had led her to believe she was going to have freedom here—not be answering to Derik, of all people.

"I'm sorry," she said, her voice dripping with sarcasm. "I didn't know I needed your permission to do my job. Deputy Director Irvin asked me to come back on personally. He never said I needed to answer to you—we're supposed to be equals now. And I definitely didn't know about any 'conditions' you had set."

"Yes, equals," Derik said. "You need to respect our partnership. And right now, you're not doing that."

She bit her tongue. "It wasn't about shunning you, Derik, or ignoring our partnership. It was just about getting the information in a timely manner, and I was on my way."

He seemed to deflate, taking in her words. "Even still, I wanted us to go together. You should've called me."

She'd never known Derik to be the emotional type or get hung up on a detail like this. Morgan knew she should drop it, but she couldn't resist: "Look, if this is about last night, then—"

Derik held up a hand. "We don't have to talk about that."

Morgan clenched her jaw, feeling the tension between them grow thicker. She had no idea how to diffuse the situation, so she decided to focus on the case instead.

"Okay, let's talk about the garden. It's a possible lead, right?" she said, hoping to steer the conversation away from their personal issues. "It's possible that Jim Alba isn't even our guy, and if that's the case, then that means people are still in danger."

Derik gave a curt nod. "Yeah, we should look into it. I'd like to see it myself, but—"

Just then the door burst open, and Amy, the intern, came flying in with a shocked expression on her face. "Agents Cross and Greene, you need to come quick. We just got a call."

"What's going on?" Morgan stepped up, her pulse racing through her chest.

Amy swallowed. "Someone broke into the maze at the botanical gardens."

***

Morgan's eyes darted around the botanical garden, taking in the brilliant hues of the exotic plants and flowers. She could see the maze winding through the grounds, and the birds chirping as they flitted through the air, almost making the place peaceful. But right now, mazes in this city were anything but a fun time.

No, the police had been ordered to keep a close eye on all of them, and apparently, this one had an intruder.

Morgan pushed past the row of police with Derik right behind her, stopping at the entrance of the maze. "Have you found him yet?" she asked an officer.

"Not yet," he said. "We sent a team in, but this maze is huge—we were standing by for more orders."

"Good, then you're with us," Morgan said, twirling her finger in the air, gathering three policemen with her. She nodded at Derik, hoping they could put their little argument earlier on ice so they could catch this son of a bitch.

If someone was breaking into the maze, then Morgan had a feeling it wasn't just for fun. Maybe it really was the Maze Killer, and Jim Alba was innocent after all—guilty only of being a terrible husband and father but not necessarily a killer.

Morgan didn't know, but she intended to find out. The morning sun scorched down on her as she made her way through the maze, leading the team into the unknown.

The team was on high alert, but Morgan could tell they were finding it hard to keep their eyes open, even as they moved forward. The maze was infuriating in its complexity, and it was disorienting as well. It would be easy for anyone to get lost in there.

And that was exactly what Morgan was afraid of.

Morgan kept her eyes open, her hands ready to pull out her gun at a moment's notice. The air smelled of fresh soil and green plants—and blood. It was a scent that Morgan knew all too well. She glanced at Derik, who gave her a knowing nod.

Morgan's heart sped up, her body tense as she led the group deeper into the maze. She bit her lip, keeping to the right of the pathway, her hand hovering just above her gun. She could feel her pulse beating in her throat, her skin covered in a thin sheen of sweat.

The sound of their footsteps seemed to echo off all sides of the hedges, as if they were being followed. Morgan turned around, but there was no one there. The prickle of anger made her skin erupt into goose bumps. She knew this killer would show up, she'd just had a feeling. But she didn't know where.

She looked up, realizing there was a long split in the hedge, facing a narrow pathway.

And there, up ahead, was a man.

A tall, skinny man looked back at them in shock, giving them no time to even process it. Before Morgan could react, he dashed away.

She ran after him.

"Cross, hold up!" Derik shouted, but Morgan sprinted ahead, leaving the rest of the team behind. During her time in prison, she'd mastered her speed, having spent afternoons outside in the field, doing laps the entire time, at every chance she got. It was the only saving grace in prison; the fact that she could still work on her body and make herself stronger and faster than she ever was before.

Morgan chased the suspect through the maze, jumping over low walls and ducking under high branches. The man was fast, but Morgan was faster. She could see him up ahead, his long strides covering the distance between them in a second.

Just as Morgan was about to catch up with him, he stopped abruptly, pointing his gun straight at her. His eyes were wide and wild, and his finger flexed around the trigger. Fear flooded through Morgan's veins as she stared down the barrel of the gun.

It was a sobering moment—a reminder that anything could go wrong and end her life at any time, especially in this line of work.

But the man didn't shoot, not yet, giving Morgan a chance to compose herself. She'd been here before. She could handle it.

"Drop the weapon," she said, pointing her own gun back at him.

"I-I didn't do anything!" he shouted. "I was just—I was just following instructions!"

"What instructions?" Morgan said, her voice hard.

"I-I don't know," the man said.

"Who sent you?" Morgan said.

"I was just given instructions to go in the maze and wait for instructions," the man said, sweat trickling down his face.

Morgan frowned. "Who gave you these instructions?"

"I don't know!" the man wailed. "This isn't my fault, you can't—you can't do this! Please, just let me go."

Morgan stared at him, her jaw clenched. She knew that if she let him go, he'd just be back out there doing the same thing, or worse. No, she couldn't let that happen.

"Drop your weapon," Morgan said, her voice cold and unwavering. "Now."

He didn't; he just kept holding it up.

"Drop it," she commanded again, her voice low but forceful. "Or I'll shoot."

"It's not fair," he stammered. "It's not—"

"Cross!" Derik's voice sounded from behind.

Before Morgan could react, the suspect fired his gun right at her.

CHAPTER ELEVEN

White-hot pain seared through Morgan's thigh. Disoriented, she tried to find her bearings through the new pain and the sound of the gunshot that still resonated through her head. The sun blinded her, and the pain was so intense it nearly made her pass out.

But only for a moment.

Morgan looked down to see her pants ripped open. The bullet had only grazed her thigh, and she looked up to see the suspect trembling, his gun still on her.

"I'll shoot again!" he warned.

Anger fired through her. That son of a bitch had shot her. She glared at him, then dove right after him. Clearly, he was a bad shot, but he didn't try to shoot her again—this time, he dropped the gun and ran off. Morgan hobbled after, but the pain in her leg slowed her down. The adrenaline pushed her forward.

"Cross, hold up!" It was Derik. Morgan ignored him and chased after the suspect. This time, it was anger that pushed her forward.

She was sick of men like him thinking they could get away with anything, thinking they could hurt anyone without consequences. She wasn't going to let him go.

The suspect was quick, but Morgan's anger and determination made her faster. She chased him through the maze, feeling the pain in her thigh with every step. But she refused to let it slow her down. He was slower now, too, and he kept looking back in fear as Morgan charged him.

She was going to catch this son of a bitch and make him pay for what he had done to her. She pushed herself to run faster, even as the pain in her thigh intensified. She could hear the suspect's frantic footsteps as he ran ahead, but she was getting closer.

And then she finally caught up to him. Morgan hurled herself forward, taking his weight down with her.

They tumbled to the ground, rolling over and over until she was on top of him. His face was twisted in fear and pain, and Morgan could see the fear in his eyes as he struggled to break free. But she held him down, pinning him to the ground with all her strength.

"You shouldn't have shot me," Morgan growled, her voice low and dangerous.

"I'm sorry," the man whimpered. "Please, let me go!"

Morgan shook her head. "It's too late for that."

She reached for her handcuffs and quickly cuffed the man's hands behind his back. She stood up, looking down at him with cold eyes.

"You're under arrest," she said, her voice firm.

The man stared up at her, fear in his eyes. "What are you going to do to me?"

Morgan didn't answer, just turned back as she heard the footsteps of her team quickly arriving. They were all out of breath, Derik included. He scowled at the scene as he took it in.

"Go on," Morgan said to the officers behind him, "he's already finished."

The officers took the suspect and carried him away, navigating toward the exit of the maze. Now that the adrenaline had worn off, the pain shot up Morgan's leg again. She looked down to see blood pooling through her dark pants, creating a giant splotch.

"Jesus, Cross," Derik said, stepping up to her.

"I'm fine."

But her head was getting woozy. She tried to ignore it, to look strong. But Derik clearly didn't buy it, because he came over and forced her to use him as a crutch. Morgan's face burned at the feeling of his body pressing against hers, both familiar and unfamiliar.

"I can walk myself," Morgan uttered, trying to push Derik away, but he wouldn't let her go. The truth was that she didn't mind the extra weight taken off as they hobbled away, but it felt awkward taking Derik's help after everything that had happened.

"What the hell is wrong with you, Cross?" Derik said.

Morgan shot him a look. "What? I caught him."

"And you got shot," Derik said. "We're supposed to be working as a team, remember? Here you are, running off alone again."

She bit her tongue. What was she supposed to say? She was determined to catch this guy, and after ten years alone in a cell, surrounded only by other inmates, maybe she had lost a lot of her team spirit. It didn't feel as natural to work alongside Derik now, not like it had before.

Derik sighed, clearly still frustrated with her. "You should have waited for backup. You could have been killed."

Morgan turned away. "But I wasn't."

"That's not the point," Derik argued. "You can't just go charging in without thinking about the consequences."

Morgan gritted her teeth. She didn't want to argue with him, not now, even though it pissed her off that he kept lecturing her, as if she were a rookie and not a seasoned, forty-year-old agent. Still, her leg was throbbing, and she just wanted to get this guy dealt with.

"All right," she said, "I'm sorry."

"It's okay," he said, "just—let me help you, Morgan."

Morgan nodded, biting her lip. She didn't like feeling weak in front of Derik, or anyone for that matter. But she couldn't deny that the pain was becoming unbearable. It was a relief when they finally made it to the ambulance waiting for them outside the maze. At the same time, she knew what this meant: she'd have to go get checked out instead of interrogating that bastard, and the thought made her skin crawl.

"C'mon," Derik said, "you're getting in the ambulance, Cross. I can't have my partner injured."

Morgan gritted her teeth. It wasn't about rejecting help now but saving time. She wanted to say no, but how could she when that pool of blood on her leg was only getting bigger? She probably needed stitches.

"I need to talk to him with you," she said. "I can deal with the wound later."

"I can interrogate him myself," Derik said. "I'm sure they can get you patched up within an hour, then we can be back in the field."

She sighed, hating the fact that he was right. Morgan had always been stubborn, but she felt it now, more than ever.

Still, she had to recognize when she was down for the count.

Morgan just nodded, not trusting herself to speak.

Derik helped her into the ambulance, and Morgan was glad to see that the paramedics didn't need to be told what to do. One of them began cutting off Morgan's pant leg.

"It's okay," the other one said, "you're a tough lady. We'll get this patched up."

"Thanks," Morgan mumbled. Despite the pain in her thigh, she felt a strong sense of relief.

Now, it would be Derik interrogating the suspect, and her leg would get a chance to heal.

Morgan closed her eyes, but her mind raced. She couldn't shake the feeling that she was missing something. Something important.

She had caught the suspect. That was the main thing. She didn't need to get any more than that, right? It was all she needed to be able to go head-to-head with the FBI. She didn't need that training to become the best. She was enough on her own.

No, she wasn't.

The truth was that Morgan missed the feeling of being a part of a team. She missed the feeling of trust and friendship, the feeling of having people she could rely on no matter what. She used to be more in line, more likely to trust and rely on others, but all of that had changed now. She'd thought she trusted Derik, but maybe some part of her did feel like she couldn't rely on him, that she was better off doing things on her own.

For now, she was stuck, forced to trust him. She just hoped he'd get the right information out of the suspect. He'd said something about being "given orders."

Given orders by who?

***

Derik faced off against the suspect in the interrogation room back at HQ. The man trembled, shaking like a leaf, his eyes looking everywhere but at Derik.

It turned out that his name is Steven Jolie, and he seemed like an innocuous person on paper. No criminal record, no history of severe trauma or mental health. By all accounts, he seemed like a normal person, so why did he break into the maze, and why was it worth shooting a federal agent over?

Part of him wished Morgan were here to talk this guy into speaking, but at the same time, Derik needed a break from her. Morgan was being headstrong and reckless on this case. And when she'd kissed him, he wasn't sure how to feel about it. His body had reacted at first, and he'd kissed her back, but this was Morgan Cross they were talking about. He felt like she was maybe using him, as he'd never noticed her attracted to him when they were partners ten years ago. Maybe she was just drunk and looking for someone, and Derik filled that void.

He shook his mind away from it, focusing on the case.

"Come on, Steven," he said, "I need you to talk, man. I'm sure your life's worth more than whatever this is."

"I told you," Steven stammered, "I just followed instructions. That's all."

"Instructions from who?" Derik said, not buying this at all. Steven was all shaky and paranoid, maybe even on drugs.

"It ... it was a man," he said. "I didn't know him, I swear. But he threatened me. He said I had to wait in the maze, and that you'd come for me. He said I had to shoot and run."

Derik leaned back in his chair. This was all sounding ridiculous.

"A man, huh?" Derik said skeptically. "Can you describe him?"

"He was tall, had a beard, and wore a black hoodie," Steven said, still shaking.

Derik wrote down the description, but he doubted it would lead anywhere. It was too vague.

"And what did this man look like? Did he show you anything that could identify him? A tattoo? Something more specific?" Derik asked.

Steven shook his head. "No, he was just ... there. And then he was gone. It was dark. I couldn't really see him all that well."

Derik sighed, feeling like he was hitting a dead end. This man Steven spoke of probably didn't even exist. The way Steven had described the man, it sounded too generic, too much like a made-up story. But why would he do that? What did he have to gain?

"Look, Steven," Derik said, "you're already under arrest for shooting a federal agent. This is the end of the road for you, so let's just talk candidly, okay?"

Steven blinked, still shaking. His face had gotten paler since they brought him in, backdropped by the lights in the interrogation room. "I-I swear. I don't know anything. Please." He shuddered. "Oh, man, I don't feel so good."

And then, without warning, Steven suddenly collapsed to the floor. He lay there, twitching and convulsing as Derik ran to his side in alarm. His skin was cold and clammy to the touch, and Derik could feel a fever radiating from him. Panic flooded Derik's chest.

"Help!" he shouted, and two guards ran into the room. Everything sped by Derik in slow-motion. The guards called in emergency paramedics. Soon, the room buzzed with activity as paramedics worked hurriedly to revive him while Derik looked on helplessly. Everything felt like a blur as he watched them perform CPR, desperately trying to get Steven's heart beating again.

But it was no use.

Steven Jolie was dead.

CHAPTER TWELVE

"What do you mean he's dead?" Morgan asked, storming through headquarters after Derik. Her leg throbbed from the stitches she'd just been given, but they'd patched her up good and sent her on her way. Or, she forced her way out, more like. As soon as the last stich was on, Morgan had gone on her way, buying a new pair of pants from the hospital gift shop on the way out. The denim fabric of the jeans, probably made for someone twenty years younger than her, irritated her wound, but she didn't care.

She couldn't believe what she was hearing.

Derik had a perturbed look on his face as he looked back at her and said, "He's dead, Morgan. What else do you want me to say?"

She stopped in the hallway, hands on her hips. Derik breathed out through his nose as he faced her.

"I leave for an hour, and a suspect dies in custody," Morgan said. "How did this happen?"

"We don't know." Derik turned into the briefing room, and Morgan followed after, letting the door close behind her. "We're waiting on toxicology and an autopsy. Maybe he had a heart attack."

Morgan bit her lip, thinking. Or maybe it was something else. They were dealing with poison in this case, after all.

"Did he say anything?" Morgan asked. "Do you think he was the Maze Killer?"

"I don't know," Derik said. "He said that he met with a man who coerced him into meeting us in the maze and shooting. It sounds like we were his targets." Derik's eyes flashed to Morgan. "Maybe you were his target."

She balked at that. "Me?"

Derik nodded, taking a seat on the other side of the briefing room. "This guy could have been after you," he said. "The guy who Steven allegedly met with."

"Do we know if that guy is even real?" Morgan asked.

"No. But he described him as 'tall and with a beard.' That's all I could get out of him."

Morgan leaned back on the table, taking the weight off her sore leg. This was a mess. But she doubted that this Steven guy was the real Maze Killer.

"Maybe his story is true," Morgan said. "Maybe someone really did threaten him."

"Even still, we have no way of knowing who that person could be."

Morgan sighed, running a hand through her hair. "We need to find out who this mystery man is. There has to be some lead."

Derik nodded. "I agree. But for now, we need to find out what the hell killed Steven."

"If it was the same poison that killed the others, then ..."

"Then we'll know it really was the Maze Killer who met with Steven and threatened him."

"Right."

The room fell into silence. A few moments later, the two were interrupted when Forbes, one of the lab techs, walked in. Morgan thought he looked more nervous than usual, his face pale and eyes wide.

"What's going on?" Morgan asked.

"Well, it's just ... it's just ..." Forbes trailed off, unable to finish his sentence.

"Spit it out, Forbes," Derik said.

"We found traces of the Bleeding Woodbine in Steven's blood," he uttered. "He was murdered."

Morgan's stomach fell to the floor. Their worst fear had been realized. It wasn't Steven, and it wasn't Jim Alba either.

The Maze Killer was very much still alive, active, and out there.

Morgan's head spun. "Thanks, Forbes. You can go."

The tech disappeared, leaving Morgan and Derik in a tense silence. Morgan's mind raced. This was a complete change in MO. The Maze Killer had killed women before and left them in the mazes. He had never killed a man, nor had he done so like this, sending him out and ordering him to shoot whoever he came in contact with. The killer was getting bold, careless even, but Morgan still had no clue who this guy was or what he wanted. This recent development complicated things even more.

She knew that they had to get a grip on this situation fast. The Maze Killer was still out there, and he was getting more dangerous every day. The team had to be careful if they wanted to catch him. She didn't want to end up like Steven Jolie, or any of the other women that the Maze Killer had killed.

"We need to find out who this guy is and fast," Morgan said, breaking the silence. "He's getting more reckless, and we don't know what his next move will be."

Derik nodded, deep in thought. "It's like he's taunting us, daring us to catch him."

Morgan sighed. "Well, he won't be taunting us for long." She looked at Derik. "We need to step up our game, Derik. We need to catch him before he kills again."

Derik frowned. "But how? We don't even know who we're looking for."

He had a point. Morgan was at a loss.

"I'll talk to the techs and see if they can trace the source of the Bleeding Woodbine," Derik said. "In the meantime, you should rest your leg. You're in no condition to be running around after a killer."

"I'm not sitting this one out, Greene," she said.

"Then keep working, but let me do the walking around."

"Since when did you start babying me so much?"

"I'm not babying you. I'm just looking out for you."

"Why? You think I can't handle myself?"

"I know you can handle yourself, Morgan," Derik said, his voice softening. "But you also just got stitches in your leg, and you need to take it easy."

Morgan sighed. "Fine," she said. "I'll stay put for now. But you better keep me updated on what you find out."

"Of course," Derik said. "I always do."

"I'll keep looking here, see if we can get a hit on whomever Steven met with."

Morgan watched as Derik left the briefing room, feeling a sense of frustration wash over her. She hated feeling helpless, especially when there was a killer out there on the loose. She knew that they had to catch this guy before he hurt anyone else, but she felt like they were running out of time.

She leaned back in her chair, trying to clear her mind. She closed her eyes and took a deep breath, trying to calm the racing thoughts in her head.

According to his statement, Steven had met with someone the previous night. If they tracked Steven's financial records, they might come up with something that could pinpoint his location for the night. It was a start.

She grabbed her laptop and opened it, going into the financial records to see what Steven had been up to leading up to his death.

She opened up Steven's latest credit card bill, checking to see where he'd been shopping. She noticed nothing unusual, just the usual stuff for a guy in his mid-twenties, nothing that seemed too out of place. No unusual places, nothing suspicious.

She stared at Steven's financial history, searching for whatever she could find. She began to question what she was doing. This wasn't helping. She needed to find some way to track Steven's location the night he met with the mystery man. They needed to find this guy, and fast. But everything Morgan did led nowhere, and her resolve was beginning to die. Much of the day had slipped away, but she'd spend the rest of it researching if she had to.

As she did, her mind wandered back to Steven, to their interaction earlier that day. He'd seemed terrified and then he'd shot her. Apparently, the man who'd threatened him had demanded that he do it. Derik's words resurfaced in her mind:

"Maybe you were his target."

***

Morgan was unnerved as she drove home, taking in the city lights now that the sun had set. Derik had mostly gone AWOL, only checking in to inform her that he'd found nothing new. She'd informed him that she'd been looking but had hit a brick wall too.

Now, it was late, her leg was still sore, and she needed to call it a night. She'd be no use if she couldn't get some sleep.

As she drove, though, she kept feeling like someone was watching her. She passed it off to blood loss and tiredness, but she kept checking her rear-view mirrors, a sense of paranoia gripping her.

Eventually, she reached her place, parking in the driveway and becoming extra cautious as she walked up to the front door. She grabbed her keys and opened it quickly, closing it securely behind her as she rushed inside. Skunk was quick to greet her, and she gently pet him. He whined, seeming unnerved as well.

"It's just your nerves," Morgan whispered to herself, trying to shake off the feeling of unease that had taken a hold of her. Skunk would have been freaking out if anyone had broken in.

She turned on all the lights in the house and checked every room for signs of an intruder, just to make sure. Nothing seemed out of place; everything was exactly where she had left it.

Morgan went into her bedroom and changed into some comfortable clothes. She fed Skunk, had a quick snack, then brushed her teeth and went back up to her room. She then flopped onto the bed with a sigh. Skunk hopped up, too, curling into a ball beside her. She knew that these feelings were irrational; no one was out there following her. But even so, she couldn't shake this feeling that something wasn't quite right ...

She checked her phone to distract herself. Nothing from Derik. Of course not. She still felt like a fool for last night's drunken kiss. What had she been thinking? Everything between them felt weird now, and even more frustrating, Derik was treating her differently, like he thought she was messy, unable to handle herself. Part of her was offended, of course, but at the same time, could she blame the guy? She had shown up to his place, half in the bag, holding a bottle of scotch, then kissed him. It was embarrassing.

Though she probably should have been productive, she decided to call it a night. She didn't want to spend the rest of the night doing nothing anyway. She kicked back, trying to sleep. She had a feeling that the morning would be a better time to search for clues.

But as she went to stick her arm under the cool side of her pillow, like she always did, something soft touched her arm beneath. Jolting back, Morgan tossed her pillow aside. Her heart sank into her stomach.

Underneath her pillow was a single white rose.

CHAPTER THIRTEEN

Derik couldn't sleep.

Staring up at the stucco of his bedroom ceiling, he couldn't stop replaying the events of the past forty-eight hours in his mind. Everything from the killings to Morgan kissing him to Steven dying in custody, right before his eyes. It all played like a cruel movie in his head, and he couldn't find the off switch.

Before Morgan, it had been years since he'd kissed a woman. He'd had a couple one-night stands since the divorce from Emma, but they were unsatisfying and often left him feeling dirty, so he'd eventually stopped bothering. Of course, he still craved the intimacy, but after having his heart thrown in the trash when Emma cheated on him, it was hard to feel that closeness again. He hadn't been lying to Morgan when he said he was out of the game, no longer looking. He'd die alone and loveless. He could handle that.

But when Morgan had kissed him, he'd felt something. The worry that she was using him, or just drunk and looking for someone, had caused him to push her away. Plus, they were partners. It couldn't happen. He'd never been kissed like that before, and it had only stoked the fire that had been smoldering between them for weeks, pushing him to pursue her. But he wouldn't.

He closed his eyes, trying to shut out the thoughts, but instead it all came rushing back. Maybe part of him had always had a crush on Morgan before she went to prison. She'd always been headstrong, smart as a whip, and above all, loyal. Loyal ...

Of course, she'd been loyal to the FBI too. She hadn't betrayed them. She shouldn't have ended up in prison.

Derik imagined all the nights she'd spent alone. How devastated she must have been to know her father died while she was behind bars, unable to even attend his funeral. It wasn't right.

Morgan was right ... he should have done more for her. He knew damn well she wasn't a betrayer. He should have kept fighting and never stopped. Instead, he'd fallen into his own routine. Got married. Got cheated on. Divorced. Became an alcoholic. Recovered from that, but the rest of him was still shattered. He buried himself in work most days and had little to no social life at all. And yet even then, Morgan had wanted to kiss him, even if it was drunk desperation.

He rolled onto his side, staring blankly at the wall now. It was too late to call her, but he couldn't shake the feeling that something was wrong. Maybe it was just his guilt, still simmering from not doing more for her when she was in prison. Or maybe it was something else.

But he couldn't put his finger on it. He tossed and turned, trying to get comfortable, but nothing seemed to be working. The events of the past few days had taken a toll on him, and he was exhausted, physically and mentally.

Eventually, he drifted into a fitful sleep, dreaming of the past and what could have been. In his dream, he was back in college, sitting next to Morgan in their criminology class. She was laughing at something he said, and he felt a rush of happiness.

But then the dream turned dark, and he was back in the present, standing over Steven's body, with Morgan nowhere to be found. Fear gripped him, and he woke up with a start, covered in sweat.

He sat up, taking deep breaths, trying to calm himself down. It was just a dream. Nothing more. But the feeling of unease remained, and he couldn't shake it. Only thinking about Morgan again was able to calm him, but in a different way.

He knew it was wrong to feel that way about her. She was his partner, and he shouldn't let his emotions get in the way of their job. But as he lay there in the dark, he couldn't help but think back to the way her lips had felt against his. He couldn't shake the memory of her soft skin, her warmth, the way she had breathed as they kissed.

Suddenly, his phone beeped, startling him out of his thoughts. AD Mueller's name spread across the screen, and he answered it. It was nearly three a.m.—he had no idea why Mueller would be calling him at this hour, but it couldn't be good.

"This is Special Agent Greene," he said.

"Greene." Mueller sounded tired but not because it was so late. His voice was grim. "I need you and Cross down at HQ stat."

Derik held his breath, waiting for Mueller to clarify.

Finally, he said:

"The Maze Killer ... he's sent in another note."

***

Derik rushed into HQ, his mind on high-alert. He'd barely gotten an hour of sleep, and now, they were back to work. He'd have to get a coffee to carry him through the day, if it were even possible.

He burst into the computer lab to see AD Mueller standing over a computer with a few young tech interns, FBI emblazoned on the backs of their shirts. The cool blue from the computer monitor lit the room, and the team gave Derik a quick glance as he rushed up behind them.

"We still don't have a trace on the email," one of the techs explained to AD Mueller.

"What's going on?" Derik asked, reading the note on the screen.

"See for yourself," AD Mueller said, his voice stern.

Derik read the words in the email, his chest in knots.

"I don't like when you mess with my designs," it read. "As punishment, for our next trial, I won't tell you the location. Solve this riddle, and you'll find your next treat: LITTLE DOE."

"Little Doe?" Derik read out loud. "What the hell does that mean?"

"We think it's a riddle of some kind," one of the techs said. "But we don't know what it means yet."

Just then the door opened, and Morgan flew in, her hair tied back with tired lines on her face. She hobbled slightly due to her injury, but Derik wasn't surprised to see her on her feet. That woman was tenacious.

"What's going on?" She asked, her eyes scanning the room.

"The Maze Killer has sent in another note," Derik explained, pointing at the screen. "And we have no idea what 'Little Doe' means."

Morgan leaned over to read the note, her eyebrows furrowing as she thought. "So, we crack the code and find the victim," Morgan said. "That's the idea?"

"You make it sound simple, Cross," Mueller said. "Any big ideas what he means by this?"

"No," Morgan said, glancing at Derik, "but I'm sure Greene and I can figure it out."

Derik nodded, his own thoughts racing. They needed to move quickly before anyone else got hurt, but he had no idea what the note meant. He hoped Morgan had some ideas.

"See to it then," Mueller said.

Morgan sped toward the exit, and Derik trailed after her. "Where are you going?" he asked.

"Briefing room," Morgan said. "I need the quiet so I can think and do some research."

Derik followed Morgan into the briefing room, and she immediately went to work on her laptop. He watched as she clicked furiously, typing away with expert speed.

"Any ideas yet?" Derik asked, curious.

"Not yet," Morgan said, her eyes locked onto the screen. "But I have a hunch ..."

Derik tried to focus, his mind racing. "Maybe it's a street name? Or a nickname?"

"Maybe," Morgan said, typing furiously on her laptop. "Or maybe it's something else entirely."

Derik leaned over her shoulder, trying to get a better look at what she was doing. He couldn't help but notice how close they were and how good she smelled.

Derik watched as Morgan began typing in a few more search terms, and then suddenly, she stopped. She looked up at him, her eyes dark and serious.

"What is it?" Derik asked.

"I think the Little Doe riddle may refer to a place," Morgan said slowly. "A doe is a deer, right? And there's one place near here that happens to have a maze. I remember it, because we had a call there before I was, well ..." she trailed off, but Derik was amazed at her memory. "Anyway, there's a school around here with the mascot of a deer. And I'm certain that's the place with the maze out back."

Derik felt a shiver run down his spine. "That sounds like the kind of place the Maze Killer would choose."

Morgan nodded, then opened up a map of the schoolyard. Sure enough, there was the maze. She looked up at him, her eyes blazing. "I think we should check it out."

Derik nodded, impressed with Morgan's quick thinking. "Let's do it," he said, grabbing his gun and following her out of the briefing room.

"Meet me in the car," Morgan said. "I'm gonna get Mueller to assemble a team to meet us there, with full sky coverage."

Derik nodded, taking off down the hall without Morgan. He stepped out into the dreary, cool night. As he made his way to the car, Derik couldn't help but feel a sense of unease in the pit of his stomach. They were walking into a trap; he just knew it. But he couldn't let his emotions get in the way of their job. They had to catch the Maze Killer before he could harm anyone else.

But nothing could ever be that simple. Derik had a feeling they were in for a long night.

Morgan joined him a moment later, a determined look on her face. She climbed into the passenger seat while Derik started the car. They drove in silence, the only sound coming from the static of the radio.

The school was just a few minutes away, but it felt like an eternity. Derik could feel his heart pounding in his chest as he parked the car outside the school gates. There was already a helicopter in the sky, illumining the darkness and creating a sound like rolling thunder in the sky.

"Ready?" Morgan asked, checking her gun.

Derik nodded, his own gun already in his hand. They both got out of the car and walked toward the school, their eyes scanning the area for any signs of movement. Some of the other field agents were already there, their flashlights moving across the field as they zeroed in from multiple directions, descending upon the maze like predators.

The school was eerily quiet, the only sound being the rustle of leaves in the wind. Derik's hand tightened around his gun as they approached the maze.

"Be careful," Morgan warned as they entered the maze. "We don't know what we're walking into."

"You're the one who got shot, remember?" Derik said.

"Yeah, well, let's not have a repeat of that," Morgan muttered.

The maze was a labyrinth of hedges, the path twisting and turning in all directions. Derik followed Morgan as she led them deeper into the maze. They were both on high alert, ready for anything. Maybe, this time, if they found the victim soon enough, there would be some hope of stopping the spread of the poison. At this point, it felt feeble to hope, but it was hope that got him through every hard case as an agent.

But as they looked through the maze, Derik and Morgan found nothing. No clues, no sign of the killer or his victim. Just an empty maze, still and silent in the night. The only thing that could be seen was dew collecting on the grass from the night's fog, shimmering in the helicopter's occasional searchlight.

Derik and Morgan continued through the maze, yet despite their best efforts, they found nothing. The Maze Killer had seemingly vanished into thin air. With every passing moment, Derik's heart sank further and further as they came up empty handed again and again.

As they turned a corner, they were suddenly confronted by a wall, with no path forward. Frustrated, Derik pounded his fist against the hedge.

Suddenly, they heard a faint rustling in the bushes behind them. They both turned around, guns at the ready. But instead of the Maze Killer, they saw a raccoon, its eyes gleaming against their flashlights. It flashed its teeth before it scurried off.

Derik let out a relieved breath as the raccoon disappeared into the brush. "Just a raccoon," he muttered.

Morgan chuckled, but it was a hollow sound. "Yeah. Just a raccoon."

They turned to leave, but Derik paused, his eyes scanning the bushes behind them. Something felt off.

"What is it?" Morgan asked, noticing his hesitation.

"I don't know," Derik said slowly. "But I feel like we're being watched."

Morgan tensed, her gun at the ready. "Let's get out of here," she said.

As they emerged from the maze, they were met by Mueller and the rest of the team. "Anything?" Mueller asked, his eyes scanning them both for any signs of trouble.

Derik shook his head, feeling defeated. "Nothing. Maybe he's not here yet."

"We should keep a team eyeing this place at all times," Morgan said. "He could be toying with us, but he could also just be waiting for his time. We can't afford to take our eyes off this maze."

"Agreed," Mueller said. “For now, let's get out of here. We need to regroup and come up with a new plan."

Derik and Morgan nodded in agreement, their exhaustion weighing heavily on them. The killer was always one step ahead of them, leaving them feeling like they were fighting a losing battle.

He was out there, somewhere in this city. Derik feared the worst—that another young woman had already been poisoned and would soon die.

CHAPTER FOURTEEN

Back at HQ, Morgan sighed in frustration as she looked over the evidence in the lab with Forbes, the young forensic tech. The guy was no older than twenty-five and carried himself insecurely, but he was good at his job. While the team kept their eyes on the school, Morgan needed to do something useful, and she figured the best she could do was look into the poison he'd been using to off his victims. The one thing that was consistent with all of them, including the man.

It was baffling to Morgan that he'd suddenly switched MOs and gone from killing red-haired women to a random man, and she was eager to find out why. Steven Jolie had been innocent, it seemed. Why did the killer bring him into it?

Forbes showed Morgan a paper that appeared to be some sort of chemical analysis. Morgan was an FBI field agent, not a scientist, so it didn't mean anything to her.

"This is the chemical compound in the Bleeding Woodbine," Forbes explained. "It contains alkaloids such as hyoscyamine, atropine, and scopolamine. That's what's responsible for the anticholinergic toxicity."

"I see," Morgan said. She had basic knowledge of toxic plants, of course, but she was no expert. This was news to her. "So, where do you think someone would get a high concentration of this stuff?"

"It's not impossible to come by naturally," he explained. "The belladonna—the Bleeding Woodbine—grows in the wild."

Talking about plants, Morgan thought back to the flower she'd found under her pillow earlier. The white rose. It had terrified her, and she'd been doing all sorts of mental gymnastics to convince herself there was another reason why it could be there. Maybe her neighbor put it there as a present. Maybe she'd somehow put it there herself. There had to be an explanation.

She pushed it away. Dealing with the Bleeding Woodbine had to come first.

"But someone would need a high concentration of it to kill so quickly, right?" Morgan said.

"In an adult woman, definitely," Forbes said. "Poisoning can take days. Unless the killer somehow began poisoning them before they realized it and timed it for them to die when he wanted them to."

Morgan lifted her head. It sounded preposterous out loud, but what Forbes had said could have some truth to it. Was it possible the killer was stalking these women, that he was known to them? She thought back to the gardener theory. With all the chaos that had gone on, they hadn't had the chance to run it down fully, but there had been no known connections between the victims, other than the unknown reason why Mia was at Grace's house. There were still so many things Morgan didn't have answers to, but she had a gut feeling that if she followed the trail of the poisonous plant, she'd find her killer at the end of it.

"There's a ton of books on this stuff at my university," Forbes said. "I used to spend hours reading up about poison and how it can affect the human body. Good to know as a forensic analyst."

"Sounds like it would be good for me to know too," Morgan said. "Know any profs from the program who might be able to help me dig up some information?"

"Yeah, call Professor Asha," he said. "She's the head of toxicology. She taught me everything I know."

Morgan thanked Forbes and quickly made her way over to her office, sliding behind her desk to grab her phone. Her heart was racing as she dialed Professor Asha's number. After a few rings, the professor answered.

"Hello?" a tired, female voice said.

"Professor Asha, this is FBI Special Agent Morgan Cross. I'm working on a case and was hoping to pick your brain about something."

"Of course, what can I help you with?" Asha said, sounding more alert.

Morgan explained the situation to Asha, detailing the Bleeding Woodbine poison and the mystery surrounding the killer's identity.

"I see," Asha said thoughtfully. "Bleeding Woodbine is a powerful poison. A high concentration of it can be lethal. Whoever is doing this knows what they're doing."

"Do you think it's possible that the killer is stalking these women, poisoning them before they realize it?" Morgan asked.

"It's definitely possible," Asha said. "Someone who knows about plants and their effects could easily get their hands on Bleeding

Woodbine. And by poisoning them slowly, the killer could control when they die."

Morgan felt a chill run down her spine. The thought of the killer stalking his victims, watching them suffer before their ultimate demise, made her sick to her stomach.

"You're welcome to come down to the lab, Special Agent Cross," Asha said. "I'm working a late night, and we have plenty of research here for you to view."

"Thank you, Professor," Morgan said with relief. "I'll be down there shortly; it would be great to have a look at the research."

***

Morgan hadn't been to a university in a long time. The lab was located in the basement of the university, and as Morgan made her way down the dimly lit stairwell, she couldn't help but feel a little uneasy, her mind still swimming on the white rose beneath her pillow. She'd felt like she was being watched before—maybe, somehow, she was. But it didn't make sense. How could someone have gotten into her house?

She pushed the thought aside and made her way to the lab entrance. It was dead quiet at this hour, only the sounds of Morgan's shoes clacking over the floor. She ignored the pain in her leg as she followed the instructions Professor Asha had given to her. She found a tall, lithe woman with brown skin and a long, dark braid running down her back. Professor Asha smiled at her and held out a hand.

"Special Agent Cross?"

"Yes," Morgan said, "thanks for meeting with me."

"Not a problem at all," Professor Asha said. "I'm glad to help. I have a few things I'd like to show you." She led Morgan to a table filled with books and papers. "This is everything we have on the plant in the last five years. All my students' work as well. Feel free to take a look."

Morgan sat down at the table and began to read through the papers. She couldn't help but feel overwhelmed by the amount of information in front of her. The sound of Professor Asha typing on her computer was the only noise in the room.

Morgan read through papers and studied diagrams for hours, but found nothing note-worthy. She looked over the research, trying to make sense of it all. Asha had written detailed accounts of her experiments and the results she'd gotten. Morgan read them carefully but still couldn't draw any connections between the victims and her work.

As the night went on, Morgan's eyes began to droop with exhaustion. She rubbed them wearily as she pushed away from the table. It was getting into the morning now, and her day was only just beginning, despite the fact that her sleep had been abruptly interrupted by the news earlier.

Just as she was thinking of giving up, a paper she had missed caught her eye. She pulled it closer to her, only to see it was about a potential fast-acting antidote to the poison.

Not only that, but it had been written recently—only a month ago. By someone named Professor George Johnson.

"Professor Asha." Morgan lifted her head, and Asha looked over at her. "Do you know a Professor George Johnson?"

"Of course," Asha said, "he is my colleague. You saw his paper? He's a brilliant man."

Morgan nodded. "I did. Do you think I could meet with him?"

"Absolutely," Asha replied. "I can give you his contact information. But why do you want to meet with him?"

Morgan hesitated before answering. "I think he might have some information that could help with my case."

Asha gave her a curious look but nodded. "I'll email you his information right away. And if you need anything else, don't hesitate to contact me."

"Thank you, Professor," Morgan said with a grateful smile as she made her way out of the lab. She felt a glimmer of hope that maybe she was getting closer to finding the killer.

***

Professor Asha had given Morgan Professor Johnson's contact information, but Morgan didn't contact him herself. Instead, she looked into his schedule, only to see that he happened to have a lecture that morning.

Now, Morgan stood at the back of the lecture hall, watching as he talked at the front of the room, his students watching intently. If he truly did know of an antidote, it could be hugely helpful for them, especially for if—when—the Maze Killer struck again. So far, he hadn't shown up, and the police and FBI were watching other mazes across the city too. But they couldn't watch them forever. He would strike again, and they needed to be ready.

Morgan listened as Professor Johnson spoke, his voice smooth and confident as he explained the properties of various plants and how they could be used to make antidotes for poisons. Finally, the lecture ended, and students began to gather their things and leave the lecture hall.

Morgan quickly made her way down to the front of the room, not wanting to lose sight of Professor Johnson. As he finished packing up his things, Morgan approached him, her FBI badge displayed prominently on her jacket.

"Excuse me, Professor Johnson?" she said, her voice firm and professional.

The professor looked up at her, his dark eyes taking in her badge. "Yes, how can I help you?"

"I wanted to talk to you about a paper you published regarding the Bleeding Woodbine and a potential fast-acting antidote."

Professor Johnson's face reddened, and he turned away. "I'm sorry, but if you actually read the paper, you'd know the research is very speculative and in its early stages. Very inconclusive. I'm afraid I can't help you."

"Please," Morgan said. "There has to be something you can do."

"I'm sorry, but I don't know what you want from me," he said, gathering up his books. "I'm very busy today. If you'd like, we can meet later, but I have to rush to my next lecture."

Morgan felt a twinge of frustration at his reluctance to help, but she knew better than to push too hard. Instead, she handed him her card.

"Please, if you think of anything or have any information, don't hesitate to contact me," Morgan said, her tone gentle. "It could be important to an ongoing investigation."

Professor Johnson hesitated before nodding and taking the card. "I'll keep that in mind," he said.

Morgan watched as he hurried out of the lecture hall, her mind already racing with possibilities. Maybe he was just busy, but something about his behavior made her suspicious. She knew that if she wanted answers, she would have to dig deeper.

"Excuse me?" a soft voice suddenly said, and Morgan turned to see a young woman, holding a binder to her chest, blonde hair falling over her shoulders. She had still been in the room, apparently, and she approached from the top row of chairs.

"Yes?" Morgan said.

She bit her lip as she came up to Morgan, glancing around. The room was empty now.

"Is everything okay?" Morgan asked, concerned. This girl seemed nervous about something.

"I heard you talking to the professor," she peeped. "I saw you were FBI ..."

Morgan squared her shoulders, fully attentive now. "Yes, that's right. I'm looking into the case of the Maze Killer. I'm sure you've heard of it."

"I have," the girl said. "And I wanted to talk to you about the professor."

"Why?" Morgan said, her heart pounding.

The girl bit her lip, then said, "Because he's not who he says he is."

CHAPTER FIFTEEN

The girl—Tiffany, she'd called herself—sat across from Morgan in a café off campus. It was the only place Morgan could convince her to go to talk more in-depth about whatever it was she had to say about Professor George Johnson. The aroma of freshly ground coffee beans filled the air, along with the sweet scent of pastries and hot chocolate. It reminded Morgan of a hipster hangout, the type of café she'd never have been caught dead in when she was in the FBI academy. The café was filled with people wearing vintage clothes, thrifted shirts, and dark jeans. It had a rustic aesthetic, with an old school record player playing classic rock music in the corner. At the counter, baristas were busy making intricate coffee drinks with almond milk and honey. The walls were adorned with vintage posters and prints of local artwork. But if this was where Tiffany felt comfortable, then Morgan could deal with it.

"So," Morgan said, "you mentioned the professor isn't who he says he is. Can you elaborate on that please?"

Tiffany trembled, biting her lip as she looked around. Her blue eyes caught the light that poured in through the windows. "Y-yes. It's just—I knew one of the girls who died."

"What?" Morgan said. She hadn't expected this.

"Yes, Nelly Swanson," Tiffany said. "She was ... the first one."

Morgan remembered. That was when the police were still in charge of the case, and it had happened a couple weeks before the current timeline had escalated.

"She went here," Tiffany said. "She was in one of my classes with Professor Johnson. She's ... one of many girls who complained about him."

Morgan's heart raced. She hadn't expected this turn. But if Nelly was the first victim, maybe that was what had turned him onto his spree. Maybe he'd started chasing the high of that first victim, and that was what triggered him to keep killing red-haired women. It didn't explain the man, Steven, but still. George had acted very sketchy when Morgan had tried to talk to him earlier.

Tiffany's story could check out. But she needed to know more.

"Complained about what?" Morgan asked.

Tiffany hesitated, fidgeting with her binder. "Um, well, things started out small. He would make comments about our appearance or what we were wearing. Sometimes, he would ask us to stay after class, and then ... he would say things that made us uncomfortable."

Morgan's heart sank. It sounded like Professor Johnson had been sexually harassing his students.

"It got worse," Tiffany continued. "He started touching us. Nothing overtly sexual, but ... just enough to make us feel violated. Nelly was one of the worst affected. She told me she wanted to report him, but ... she was scared."

Morgan felt a wave of anger wash over her. How many other girls had gone through this? How many other girls had been too scared to speak up?

"Did Nelly ever confront him?" Morgan asked.

Tiffany shook her head. "No. She wanted to, but ... she was afraid of what he might do. She was ... she was scared he might hurt her. But she was going to come forward. Then she died, and this whole Maze Killer craziness started."

Morgan felt a swell of anger. This professor had been using his position of authority to take advantage of vulnerable young women. And now, he was a suspect in a string of murders.

"Do you have any proof of this?" Morgan asked.

Tiffany shook her head. "No ... But I heard them talk about it. I know it's true."

Morgan nodded, understanding. She took out her notepad and jotted down some notes. She believed Tiffany's story, without a doubt. But that didn't necessarily make George the killer.

"I was thinking, maybe he somehow overheard that she was gonna come forward," Tiffany went on. "And that's ..." She bit her lip. "That's why I became too scared to talk too. But when I saw you, I knew I had to say something. For Nelly. And all those other girls."

Morgan nodded. "You did the right thing," she said. "Thank you for coming forward. I'll look into it and see what I can find."

Tiffany nodded, her eyes filling with tears. "Please. Stop him. Before anyone else gets hurt."

Morgan reached across the table and placed a hand on Tiffany's arm. "I will," she promised. "I'll do everything in my power to make sure justice is served."

As Tiffany left the café, Morgan sat back and closed her eyes, thinking. She had a new lead now, and it was the most promising one yet. She couldn't wait to get started on investigating Professor Johnson. But before she did, she needed to make a call.

She picked up her phone and dialed a number. "Hello?" a smooth voice answered.

"Greene," Morgan said, "I've got a lead. You need to hear this one."

***

Derik was on his way, but Morgan couldn't afford to wait. Johnson knew the FBI was here—he might already be running. When that occurred to her, she gathered her things as fast as she could and zipped out of the café into the sunny morning. She dashed across the street and to the university campus. If she were lucky, then Johnson would still be around here somewhere.

As she entered the building where Professor Johnson's office was, Morgan couldn't help but feel a sense of urgency. She knew that time was of the essence, and that every minute counted. She had to find Johnson before he slipped away.

As she walked down the hallway, she noticed that the door to Johnson's office was slightly ajar. Morgan's heart quickened as she pushed it open and stepped inside.

The room was dimly lit, with only a few rays of sunlight filtering through the blinds. There was no sign of Johnson anywhere. The urge to rifle through his desk was strong, but she needed to catch him physically first. She left his office, navigating her way through the university. In some ways, it felt like a maze too.

She stopped students as she hurried past them, asking, "Have you seen Professor Johnson? Professor George Johnson—is he still here?"

Most of them shook their heads, confused and bewildered.

But one student, a young man with curly hair and glasses, pointed toward the end of the hall. "Yeah, he was heading toward the exit just a minute ago. I think he was in a hurry."

Morgan thanked him and rushed toward the exit, her heart racing with adrenaline. She was getting closer. She could feel it.

As she burst through the doors of the university, she saw him. Johnson was walking away, his back to her, his hands shoved in his pockets. He was wearing a dark trench coat that flapped in the wind. His hair was tousled, and he looked like he was in a hurry as he made his way into the parking lot.

Morgan sprinted after him, closing the distance between them. "Professor Johnson!" she called out.

He turned around, his eyes widening in surprise. Before Morgan could stop him, he dashed toward the red car right in front of him, fumbling for his keys.

"Stop!" Morgan shouted.

But it was too late. Johnson had already unlocked the car and hopped in, starting the engine with a roar. Morgan watched helplessly as he slammed down his foot on the accelerator and drove off, tires squealing in protest. She cursed under her breath as she ran after him, but it was too late. He was gone.

No, not gone—just driving away. Morgan dashed across the parking lot toward her own car. Pain shot up her leg, but she kept pushing on. She had to. She couldn't let him get away.

Morgan fished out her car keys from her pocket and fumbled with them to unlock the door. Once she was inside, she started the engine and peeled out of the parking lot in hot pursuit. She was determined to catch up with Johnson and put an end to his killing spree once and for all.

As Morgan raced down the road after Johnson, her mind raced with thoughts of all the victims he had claimed. Nelly, Steven, and all those other girls who had been sexually harassed by their own professor. Johnson was a monster, and he needed to be stopped.

As she chased him down, Morgan couldn't help but feel a sense of exhilaration. This was what she had been trained for—to go after the bad guys and catch them, no matter what it took. And she was damn good at it. She'd been off the road for too long. But even with her burning determination, Johnson had a good head start, and soon, Morgan lost sight of the back of his red car in the sea of traffic.

Morgan's heart sank as she lost sight of Johnson's car. She had to catch up, and fast. She swerved in and out of traffic, her sirens blaring, as she tried to catch a glimpse of Johnson's car. Finally, she caught a glimpse of it farther down the road, turning a corner. Morgan gritted her teeth and pushed her car to its limits, determined not to let him get away.

Morgan cursed under her breath as she weaved in and out of traffic, trying to catch a glimpse of Johnson's car. She couldn't let him get away—not now, not after everything she had learned.

She was about to give up when she saw a flash of red up ahead. Her heart leapt in excitement as she realized it was Johnson's car stopped at a red light. Morgan pulled up behind him, her tires screeching as she came to a halt.

But the person in the driver's seat looked up in shock, and it wasn't Johnson at all—it was a woman.

Wrong car.

"Damn it!" Morgan slammed her fist on the wheel, looking ahead for any sign of Johnson. But he was nowhere to be found.

She'd let him escape.

CHAPTER SIXTEEN

"For god's sake, Cross, you should've just waited for backup," Derik chastised as Morgan stood in the university parking lot, leaning against the hood of her car. Derik's car was parked next to hers, and they were both standing there to reconvene and get a hold on the situation.

She hated Derik's tone. She hated even more that she'd let Johnson get away. It was her one job to apprehend him, but she'd let him escape. Maybe Derik was right; maybe if Morgan hadn't been so overt, Johnson would have been lulled into a false sense of safety. Maybe he would have gone home to pack his things before he fled, but they'd sent a team right there, and they hadn't received a call yet.

"Yeah, I know I messed up," Morgan said. "You don't have to bust my ass about it."

Derik sighed. "Really, what were you thinking?"

"I was thinking that this guy's almost certainly our killer, and I had to catch him."

Derik shook his head. "You're too impulsive, Morgan. You have to learn to take a step back and assess the situation."

Morgan rolled her eyes. "I know that, Derik. But we can't just sit around and wait for Johnson to make his next move. We have to be proactive."

"Proactive, sure." Derik gave her a wry smile. "But not reckless."

Morgan opened her mouth to retort, but Derik held up a hand to stop her. "I'm not trying to lecture you, Morgan. I just want you to be safe. And I want us to catch this guy."

Morgan nodded. "I know, I know. I messed up. But we can still catch him. We've got the APB out and everything. He shouldn't be able to get far."

"Maybe, maybe not," Derik said. "If this really is the Maze Killer, then he's more elusive than we can give him credit for."

Morgan nodded. He was right on that.

"Still," Derik cut in, his voice softening, "this was a good lead. I'm impressed you found him so quickly. That's the Morgan Cross I know."

Morgan smiled, feeling a slight warmth in her chest. It was good to know that Derik still had faith in her, even after all this time. She knew she had messed up, but she would make sure to make it right.

"You're right, Derik," Morgan said. "I was reckless. But I won't let it happen again. I'm stressed, if you can't tell."

"I know." His eyes crinkled, and he stuffed his hands in his pockets as he looked down at the ground.

They fell into a silence. Morgan knew they had every eye in the city looking for this guy, and all they could do now was wait. But until then, Morgan could spend her time building more of a case against him and learning everything she could. That would help. But without being active on the field, she also would have more time to think about that damn rose left under her pillow. Part of her wanted to bring it up to Derik, but it felt wrong, somehow. Maybe the rose was connected in some sick way to her connection, the one who'd given her Eric Domino's name.

It was a baseless hunch, of course. It was also possible that it was left by someone more threatening than that. Someone who wanted her dead. Could it have been a warning? An innocuous white rose, left right under her pillow, waiting to be stained red ...

***

The day went by too quickly, and Morgan didn't want to spend another day in her house. With Skunk in tow, she pushed into the dark motel room. It felt safer to be here than to be at her own house, and she hated that.

But there was still no sign of Johnson. They'd found his car at the side of the road, so he must have escaped somewhere on foot. The whole thing made Morgan uneasy, but they had cops scouring the streets, looking for him. Morgan and Derik had taken part in the search earlier, too, but they had no luck. There was only so much aimless chasing Morgan could do before she had to accept that it was time to pack it in. Plus, both her and Derik had barely gotten any sleep the night before. They needed it.

Morgan locked the motel door behind her, and Skunk wagged his tail as he roamed around the unfamiliar room, taking in all its scents. The motel room was painted in a warm cream color, and the walls were adorned with vibrant wood-paneled accents. The furniture was mostly made of wood and metal, with a sofa, a bed, two chairs, and a desk tucked in the corner. A mirrored cabinet was tucked into the wall, and two nightstands sat on either side of the bed. A faint aroma of citrus and fresh flowers filled the room, but it wasn't overwhelming or unpleasant. Just normal. Morgan could get used to a few nights here.

But she hoped it wouldn't be for long.

Once they had Johnson behind bars, then she could look further into the rose. And if the rose was, somehow, left by Johnson himself, then it was all the same in the end.

Morgan sat down on the bed, Skunk jumping up to sit next to her. She leaned back against the headboard, her mind racing with thoughts of Johnson and the rose. She couldn't shake the feeling that the rose was somehow connected to Johnson, but she had no evidence to support her theory. She needed to focus on the facts, on the case at hand.

But her mind kept going back to the rose. It was so out of place, so strange. And it had been left under her pillow in her own home. How had someone gotten in without her noticing? Without Skunk noticing? It seemed impossible. Skunk would have attacked anyone who tried to get in, unless they somehow snuck inside without being noticed.

The stress from the case was getting to her, and although Morgan was tired, she couldn't rest. She needed a drink, but the last time she'd hit the bottle, she'd embarrassed herself by kissing Derik. No, she needed to handle things sober for a while, at least until she could get her head on straight.

But she couldn't just sit here. She grabbed her laptop and went back into the database, looking for more information on Eric Domino, the man who apparently didn't exist. Was her source trying to trick her? If so, why? Morgan had the sudden urge to track that man down again and demand the real name.

It wasn't like she could sleep anyway. Skunk barked as Morgan got up and put his leash back on.

"Sorry, boy," she said, "one more stop to make tonight."

***

Morgan drove her car like a viper in the night, creeping down the street she'd met the mystery man on before. She kept her eye out for a tall, lanky guy in a hoodie, the same one she'd met before. She had an idea of where he lived. She just had to wait until he came out.

In the backseat, Skunk wagged his tail, looking around for any sign of anything.

Morgan parked her car on the side of the road and waited. The darkness wrapped around them like a blanket, and she couldn't see much of anything. But she didn't have to wait long. Soon enough, she saw the man walking down the street. He had his hood up, and he moved with a quick, nervous energy.

Morgan stepped out of her car, Skunk jumping out after her. The man stopped when he saw her, and she could feel the tension in the air. "What do you want?" he asked, his voice low and menacing.

"I want to talk," Morgan said, keeping her distance. "About Eric Domino."

The man laughed, a sharp, barking sound. "I told you all I know."

"No, you didn't," Morgan said, anger boiling in her. This was her life. This was her revenge, and this guy was messing with her, giving her fake names. "Eric Domino doesn't exist, asshole. So, what's the real name?" She touched her gun, in its holster on her belt, and the man's eyes widened. She had no intention of truly using it, but a little threat couldn't hurt if it got her the truth. Reading her, Skunk gave out a warning bark.

The man raised his hands, fear on his face as he backed away. "I'm telling you the truth, that's the name of the guy. It was Eric Domino. I heard he was a buddy of a buddy, you know, selling drugs and all that, but then something weird happened. That night you were there, Eric called in to report you. Like to the cops or something."

Morgan's mind raced. Why would a drug dealer and a criminal ever call the police?

Her stomach felt sick as it dawned on her.

They might do something like that ...

If they were an undercover FBI agent.

Morgan felt sick. Was it possible someone at the very Bureau she'd dedicated her life to had betrayed her?

"No," Morgan said, "you're lying. Give me the name."

The man shook his head, his eyes darting around nervously. "I swear, that's all I know. I heard rumors he was a snitch."

Morgan's mind was spinning with the implications of what the man had just told her. If Eric Domino was really an undercover agent, that would mean that he'd been working with the FBI from the beginning. It would also mean that the FBI had been watching her the entire time.

She felt a cold sweat break out on her skin. Could she really trust anyone?

Morgan's frustration turned to anger. She had come all this way for nothing. "Fine," she said. "Get out of here."

The man turned and ran, disappearing into the darkness. Morgan watched him go, her mind racing with questions. She needed to know the real identity of this man. What if he still worked at the FBI?

What if she knew him?

Just then, her phone rang. Morgan pulled it out, still feeling numb from the dizzying revelation. It was Derik.

"Greene," Morgan said into the phone, "what is it?"

"They found him, Cross," Derik said.

Morgan looked around the dark, rundown street. The asphalt below her feet was cracked and broken, covered in debris and littered with trash. The buildings were crumbling, paint peeling off walls and windows boarded up. The street lamps were dull and duller, barely providing any light at all. Everything was shrouded in shadows, eerie and oppressive. But she felt numb. It was hard to even care about the Maze Killer right now after what she'd just learned.

"He won't talk," Derik said. He took a breath. "He said he'd only talk to you, and you alone."

She wondered why he gave a damn who he talked to, but if he wanted her, then he'd have her. "Where is he?" she asked.

"At the precinct," Derik replied. "How fast can you get here?"

Morgan's heart raced at the thought of facing Johnson again. But this time, she wouldn't let him get the upper hand. She'd make him talk, one way or another. "I'll be there in ten," she said, hanging up the phone.

Skunk jumped back into the backseat, and Morgan turned the car back toward the motel to drop Skunk off, then headed into the precinct. She couldn't shake the feeling of betrayal, but right now, catching the killer was her top priority. She'd deal with the FBI later.

But if someone truly did betray her, she'd find out who they were.

All in due time.

CHAPTER SEVENTEEN

When Morgan walked into the interrogation room, the man she saw sitting there certainly looked different from the flustered professor she'd seen at the school. An eerie calm had settled over him, and his beady, dark eyes glared at Morgan as she slid into the seat across from him.

"You came," he said.

"Of course." Morgan crossed her arms and leaned back in the chair. "Any particular reason you wanted to see me again?"

"You're the one who boldly came into my classroom and messed everything up," he said. "And I didn't expect you to chase me with your car."

Morgan laughed in a mocking way. Johnson offered a slightly amused smile back, but there was still that darkness in his eyes. Morgan couldn't forget Tiffany's statement, about how Johnson had made female students uncomfortable, going as far as to touch them without their consent. He was the lowest of the low, even if he was a "brilliant man," as Professor Asha had quoted.

"Let's just cut to the chase," Morgan said. "I know Nelly Swanson was your student. Did killing her give you the rush you needed to go after the other women?"

Johnson glowered. "I didn't kill anyone, certainly not Nelly Swanson. You don't have any proof."

"I don't need proof," Morgan said, her eyes flashing with anger. "I know it's you. And I'm going to make you pay for what you've done."

Johnson laughed, a hollow sound that made Morgan's skin crawl. "You can't make me do anything. I'm a respected member of this community. The police won't believe you."

Morgan smiled, a cold, calculating look. "I don't need the police—I'm the damn FBI. I have other means of making you talk."

Johnson scoffed. "You really think you scare me, Special Agent Cross?"

Morgan leaned even closer, her voice low and menacing. "You should be scared, Johnson. I know how it feels to be locked up behind bars, and it's cold, unforgiving, and lonely. There's no happiness there. And you'll be locked up forever."

His eyes flashed. "I didn't do it."

"You know a lot about the Bleeding Woodbine," Morgan went on. "You've studied it extensively."

"And what of it?"

"Every victim so far has had it in their system. One of those victims happens to be a student who you harassed."

"Harassed?" Johnson's face flushed, taken aback. "I never 'harassed' Nelly. What, a man gives a woman a compliment, and it is 'harassment' now? It wasn't like she was a child; she was in her thirties."

Morgan shook her head in disgust. "Complimenting someone is one thing, Johnson. But touching them, making them feel uncomfortable, that's not okay. It's harassment."

"I never touched her," he said, his eyes narrowing.

Morgan leaned forward, a fierce glint in her eyes. "Don't lie to me. I know you did. You made her feel small, scared, and vulnerable. And now, she's dead because of you."

"I didn't kill her!" Johnson shouted, slamming his hands down on the table.

Morgan leaned back, trying to calm the situation down. "Then who did? Who is the Maze Killer?"

Johnson's eyes darted around the room like he was trying to come up with a lie. "I don't know."

Morgan slammed her hand down on the table. "Don't play games with me! You just so happen to know all about this deadly plant, and one of your students dies because of it? And if you're so innocent, why did you run from me earlier?"

Johnson looked around the room, nostrils flared. Maybe it was settling in that he was screwed no matter what. "Look, I did hear rumors about what the female students were saying about me," he said. "When I heard about it, I backed off. I never meant to make them get their panties in a twist."

Morgan bit her tongue. Part of her wanted to punch this sexist asshole in his face, but she kept it together.

"It was never my attention, okay?" he said. "I thought they liked the attention. Some of them did. They'd even come to me, ask me for better grades. Sorry if I started to feel a bit powerful because of it."

Morgan's eyes narrowed, her jaw clenched tight. Johnson's words only confirmed what she already knew: he was a predator, using his power to manipulate and control those around him. "You're sick," she said, her voice cold. "And it's time for you to pay for what you've done."

"What have I done?" Johnson spat. "I haven't killed anyone! I'm not the Maze Killer!"

Morgan leaned back in her chair, studying Johnson carefully. If he was telling the truth, then who was the real killer? She couldn't shake the feeling that something wasn't adding up.

"And what about the Bleeding Woodbine?" Morgan asked, her voice low and steady. "How did it get into the victims' systems?"

Johnson hesitated almost like he was trying to come up with a lie. "I don't know," he said finally. "I swear."

Morgan leaned forward, her eyes locked on his. "You're lying," she said. "I can see it in your eyes."

Johnson shifted in his seat, unease evident on his face. "I swear, I don't know how it got there," he said. "I may have studied it, but I never used it on anyone. But ..."

Morgan raised an eyebrow.

"I might ... I might know someone who did have a particular interest in it."

"Who?"

"I'll tell you if you let me go."

Morgan laughed. A real, belly laugh. He couldn't be serious. "You're joking, right?" she said. "You could just pin it on any person to get yourself out of this chair, then run off again like a coward. You're not going anywhere."

"Then I guess you don't want to know who it was," he said, his voice taunting.

Morgan narrowed her eyes. She didn't know what kind of game he was playing here. She also had to admit that if there was even a small chance that he was telling the truth, then maybe it was worth looking into. Still, she didn't want to play into his demands. What if he truly was the Maze Killer?

Just then, there was a knock at the door. Derik poked his head in. Morgan took the hint and left Johnson, who said, "Think about it, Special Agent!" in a taunting way as she slipped out of the room.

She met Derik in the hallway. "I hope this is important," she said.

"It is. We have a problem."

Morgan's chest sank. She prayed it wasn't another victim or another note.

But Derik said, "Johnson has an alibi for the time Grace Alba was killed, when we were in the maze. He was in a lecture. Witnesses and cameras confirmed it."

Morgan's mind raced. If that were the case, then maybe Johnson was telling the truth. Then again: "We already know he can threaten people to do work for him," she said. "Remember Steven Jolie?" Plus, why would Johnson have run if he were innocent? Maybe he had just been concerned that he'd been caught for creeping on the women in general, but Morgan had a hard time buying this guy's innocence.

"Of course," Derik muttered.

"But ..." Morgan trailed off. Grace Alba's death had seemed fresh, not to mention that the killer likely had to move very quickly to evade them and bury her at the same time. She'd profiled the killer as an able-bodied man. Johnson was in his late fifties and overweight. Clumsy. He'd only been able to escape Morgan because he'd gotten in his car first.

"I don't like it, either," Derik said. "But he might not be our guy."

"I still think we need to keep an eye on him," Morgan said. She formulated a new plan. This could work to her benefit. "Okay," she said, "Johnson was trying to tell me he can give me a name to look into if I let him go. Obviously, I was not going to do that, but if we think he might not be our guy anyway, we can make it seem like we're cutting him a deal."

Derik raised an eyebrow. "What kind of deal?"

Morgan smirked. "We'll tell him we'll consider letting him go if he gives us the name of the person he thinks might have something to do with the Bleeding Woodbine in the victims' systems. We'll make him think he's getting something out of it, but when he's out, we'll keep our eyes on him. Just in case."

Derik nodded, understanding the plan. "It's risky, but it might work," he said.

"It's worth a shot. Give me a couple minutes with him."

Morgan went back into the interrogation room, where Johnson sat with a smug look on his face.

"Changed your mind, I see," he said.

Morgan didn't bother with pleasantries. "We're willing to make a deal," she said, pressing her hands on the table and looking down on him. "You give us the name of the person you think might have something to do with the Bleeding Woodbine, and we'll consider letting you go."

Johnson leaned forward, his eyes lighting up with a greedy look. "You're serious?" he said.

Morgan nodded. "Deadly serious."

Johnson's face cracked into a wide smile. "Well then, you have yourself a deal. Have a seat, Special Agent Cross."

Morgan didn't want to listen to a word he said, but she settled into the chair across from him.

"One person does come to mind," he said. "A former student of mine. A strange guy. His name was Jerry Jameson. He always had a fascination with poisons, especially Bleeding Woodbine. I caught him experimenting with it in the lab one day, and I reported him to the Dean. I thought that was the end of it, but maybe he's still up to his old tricks."

Morgan's heart raced. This was it. They finally had a lead. "Do you have any idea where he might be now?" she asked.

Johnson shrugged. "Last I heard, he dropped out of college and disappeared. But if he's still playing with poisons, I'm sure he'll turn up sooner or later."

Morgan jotted down Jerry Jameson's name on a notepad, a plan already forming in her mind. "Thank you for your cooperation," she said, standing up. "We'll take it from here."

Johnson raised an eyebrow. "So, that's it? You're letting me go?"

"A deal's a deal, Johnson," she said. "But your behavior toward your female students will be reported to the school."

Johnson's expression turned sour. "You can't prove anything," he spat. "It's all hearsay."

Morgan glared at him. "Maybe not, but it's enough to make sure you never work in education again. Something tells me the board will listen to the FBI over you."

Johnson's face went pale, and Morgan couldn't help but feel a sense of satisfaction. She had played him at his own game. As she walked out of the interrogation room, Derik was waiting for her.

"Well?" he asked.

Morgan handed him the notepad with Jerry Jameson's name. "I'm on this."

CHAPTER EIGHTEEN

Morgan sat in the briefing room alone with her laptop open and a cup of black coffee. Derik was tailing Johnson to see where he'd go next, but Morgan was happy to leave that in his hands. She needed to know everything she could about this Jerry Jameson guy, starting with everything the FBI had on him in their database.

Taking a sip of her bitter drink, she read through the file. Jerry Jameson was thirty-eight, a former student, like Johnson had said. But where he went after he dropped out of university was more cryptic. He never went back to school, and he had a history of mental illness. Morgan frowned at the screen. This was going to be a tough one to crack. She dug deeper, searching for any potential leads.

After a few minutes, she found something that caught her attention. Jameson had been arrested for possession of illegal substances two years prior. But it turned out it was just marijuana.

A couple years after that, he launched his own business. Morgan dug up old social media posts advertising none other than gardening services.

Gardening services ...

Her heart raced. She remembered the flier she'd seen on Grace Alba's fridge. The trimmed hedges, the well-maintained garden at Mia Jones's house even after her death.

Not only was Jerry Jameson previously interested in poison, but he had his own gardening business. It wasn't officially registered—in fact, it seemed he was mostly paid under the table and in cash and didn't report most of his income. He was performing shady business practices.

Morgan couldn't shake the feeling that she was onto something. She searched for any connections between Jameson and the victims by going into the victims' phone records. Grace Alba had contacted Jameson's business from her land line. Mia, Nelly, and Patty too—all four victims, at one point or another, had called Jameson's business number.

All four of them had almost certainly employed him at one point or another.

Morgan's pulse raced faster than her thoughts could keep up with. It all felt so real, like a building toppling over on her head. Jerry Jameson could answer everything—the gardening theory, the Bleeding Woodbine, and now, the connection between all four women. Maybe this was how Grace and Mia knew each other; they shared the same gardener. They could have met each other in the neighborhood and talked about it.

She was sure of it now. All four women had let Jerry into their homes.

And he had killed them.

***

Morgan held her breath as Derik drove them, full speed ahead, toward Jerry Jameson's last known location. Apparently, he was living with his sister, Mary, on the outskirts of town.

"I can't believe we didn't see this sooner," Derik said, sweat on his brow as he drove the car toward Mary's house. It was getting later into the day, and long shadows stretched over the road. It was sunny, but Morgan felt cold.

"It doesn't matter," Morgan said. "We've got him now. We'll take him in."

Derik nodded, his jaw clenched. "Let's just hope he's there."

As they pulled up to the small house, Morgan's heart raced in her chest. This was it. The moment of truth. Derik parked the car, and they both got out. As they approached the house, Morgan saw a figure in the window. She couldn't tell who it was, but her gut told her it was Jerry Jameson. She had no idea what to expect, but she knew that this was their chance to bring an end to the case.

The house's garden was immaculate, to be expected. There was a work truck in the driveway and children's toys all over the lawn. It was a remote house on a large plot of land, and the kids belonged to Jerry's sister, not him.

They crept up to the door and knocked. Morgan waited a beat—no answer—then knocked again.

Finally, it opened.

But it wasn't Jerry—it was his sister, Mary. She looked up at them with wide eyes. She had brown hair and blue eyes, looking nothing like the victims.

"Can I help you?" she asked.

Morgan flashed her badge, along with Derik.

"Is Jerry home?" she asked.

Mary frowned. Behind her, children's toys littered the grass. "My brother is out back playing with my kids. What's this all about?"

"We need to see him, ma'am," Derik said. "Please, if you could show us to him."

Mary's frown deepened, but she stepped aside and gestured for them to follow her. They walked through the house and out to the back yard, where two young children were playing on a swing set. Jerry stood back, watching them with a proud smile on his face. He looked like a normal man on the surface—tall, slim, with dark hair and a clean face. Able-bodied, that was for sure. He had the look of a worker.

When Jerry noticed Morgan and Derik, he turned to them, frowning.

"Jerry Jameson?" Morgan called out, flashing her badge, and Jerry's eyes went wide.

"Yeah?"

"We'd like to have a word with you in private, if that's okay," Morgan said. "Would you mind coming with us?"

"Why?" Jerry leaned away. "Is something wrong?"

The kids now looked on, curious, and Morgan thought about Milly, Jim Alba's daughter. She didn't want to see another kid put through something traumatic, and she hoped Jerry would just come willingly.

"If you come with us to the station, we can explain everything," Morgan said.

"The station?" Jerry frowned. "I haven't done anything illegal, have I?"

Morgan knew he had. He'd not declared all his income on his taxes, but that wasn't what this was about. Still, Jerry wasn't outright resisting, so she kept calm.

"We'll explain everything if you come with us," Morgan said.

Jerry's eyes flicked between the agents and then over to his sister and the children. He seemed to be weighing his options. Finally, he nodded and turned to Mary. "I guess I'll be back later," he said.

"Of course, Jerry," Mary said, looking worried.

Jerry followed the agents to the car, his shoulders hunched and his eyes darting around as if he expected police to be waiting for him. He got in the back of Derik's car, and Morgan and Derik hopped in the front. Morgan watched as Derik pressed the lock; it was childproof in the back, so Jerry wouldn't be able to get out if he tried.

As they drove, Morgan could see Jerry's nervousness increasing. He fidgeted in his seat, and his eyes darted around as if he were looking for a way out. Morgan could tell he was trying to come up with a story to explain everything away.

But she wasn't going to let him. She would get to the truth, no matter what it took.

***

When they arrived at the FBI HQ, Morgan and Derik led Jerry to an interrogation room. They sat down at the table, and Morgan placed a photo of the Bleeding Woodbine in front of Jerry. "Do you know what this is?" she asked.

He looked down on it, frowning. "Yeah, of course. I studied horticulture in university, before I dropped out and realized I'm really more of a hands-on worker. What's this all about?"

Morgan glanced at Derik, then said to Jerry, "We understand you had quite the fascination with the plant when you were in school."

"Did I?" Jerry frowned. "I don't think so. No more than any others. I know that shit is poisonous so you gotta be able to identify it, make sure the kids don't eat the berries."

His clueless attitude almost made Morgan believe him. Was there a chance Johnson had made the whole thing up?

"We heard from one of your former professors that you got in trouble for experimenting with the poison found in the plant," Morgan said.

"I never did that," Jerry said. "Honestly, it kind of scared me a little."

Morgan leaned back in her chair, crossing her arms. "We also know that you had access to all four of the victims' homes."

Jerry's eyes widened, and he shifted in his seat. "This is about those killings, isn't it? I was waiting for someone to talk to me."

"You were?" Morgan lifted a brow. "Then why not just come forward?"

"I was afraid it was gonna get pinned on me," he said. "I mean, four of my clients drop dead—it doesn't look good. Can you blame me for not wanting to throw myself onto the fire?" Jerry's face went pale, and he looked like he was about to be sick. "I-I didn't kill anyone," he stammered. "I swear on my life. I'm just a gardener."

Morgan sat back in her chair, considering Jerry's words. He seemed genuinely scared and confused, but he had motive and opportunity. Maybe Johnson had just thrown Jerry under the bus to get himself out, but all of this seemed too convenient.

But Morgan had to be sure. She leaned forward, fixing her gaze on Jerry's face. "Can you explain what you were doing at each of their houses?"

Jerry swallowed hard, his Adam's apple bobbing as he did so. "I was doing maintenance work on their gardens. All four of them were my clients. I was just making sure their plants were healthy and well-maintained."

Morgan narrowed her eyes, studying Jerry's face for any signs of deception.

Morgan sighed, tapping her pen against the table. "Jerry, we need to know the truth. Was anyone else involved? Did someone hire you to do this?"

Jerry shook his head vigorously. "No! I swear, I didn't kill anyone, and I don't know who did. I had nothing to do with it!"

Morgan looked at him skeptically. She had to admit that he seemed truthful, but she'd seen enough criminals to know that appearances could be deceiving. She decided to take a different approach. She leaned forward, softening her voice. "Jerry, look. We know this is tough, and we know you're scared. But we need to know the truth. We're not here to hurt you, we just want to solve this case and find the person responsible. Can you help us do that?"

Jerry looked up at her, his eyes red-rimmed. "I'll do anything to help," he said. "I swear, I didn't hurt those people. I couldn't even hurt a fly. Whoever's doing this—it's not me."

Morgan glanced at Derik. She felt like this was going nowhere, and they needed to regroup, rethink their strategy. She stood up and said, "Give us a moment, please."

Jerry said nothing, just sulked in the chair. Morgan and Derik left the room, meeting in the hallway.

"What are you thinking?" Derik asked. "You don't really believe this guy."

"I don't know," Morgan said. "All the evidence points to him. He's the one guy we can link to every person. But we don't know if Johnson was making up the Woodbine detail."

The thought that Johnson really was the real killer, and they'd let him go, made her skin burn. Her head spun. This couldn't be it.

Just then, AD Mueller appeared up the hall, looking flustered, his face red and angry. Morgan knew that look—something was wrong.

"Cross," Mueller said, "I need you to come to my office now. Alone."

CHAPTER NINETEEN

Morgan followed AD Mueller into his office, curious why Derik wasn't invited in too. She was sure it had to be about the case, but something in Mueller's standoffish demeanor made her feel like it was more than that. It almost reminded her of how she'd been treated when she was sent to prison. Like she'd done something wrong, when to the best of her knowledge, she hadn't.

Mueller closed the door behind them and went behind his desk. "Have a seat, Cross."

She did. Mueller looked at his computer screen before he turned it to Morgan.

Her heart sank to the floor.

On the screen were hazy, faraway pictures of Morgan with Skunk—and that connection she'd met in the rough end of town, the one who'd given her Eric Domino's name.

Morgan could hardly process what she was seeing. Someone had been following her. Those feelings of paranoia were real. Someone was following her and taking pictures of her, and now, those pictures were on AD Mueller's computer.

"Sir, what is this?" Morgan asked.

"I think you can see what it is," Mueller said, his voice cold.

"Who sent you these?"

"That's beside the point. Who is this man, Cross? Our data tells us his name is Clancy Smith, and he's a damn drug dealer. Why the hell are you meeting with him? Do we need to pass you through a drug test?"

"No!" Morgan exclaimed, mortified. Of course, she hadn't been buying drugs, but her real reason wasn't so easy to explain, either. She was being backed into a corner, and she had to explain something. "Look," she said, "I was following a tip I got regarding what happened that night. The night I was arrested. I'm still trying to piece together what happened, sir."

"That doesn't explain who this is," AD Mueller said. "You're risking the FBI's reputation with these shady meetings. Clearly, you're not as secretive as you thought."

Anger flashed through Morgan. Mueller had no idea what she'd gone through. "I won't apologize for my sources, sir," she said, "not if they get me closer to the truth."

"You are not above the law, Cross," Mueller said.

"I know that, sir," Morgan replied, trying to keep her voice steady. "But I also know that sometimes, to catch a criminal, you have to get your hands dirty. I'm not doing anything illegal; I'm just trying to find the truth."

Mueller looked at her for a long moment, his expression unreadable. "I won't have it. If you want to find out what happened that night, do it by the books. But honestly, Cross, if I were you? I'd let it go. You've already spent ten years locked up. Don't let yourself be punished for it now that you're out."

Morgan felt a knot form in her stomach. She couldn't let it go. Not when there were still unanswered questions about that night. Not when she knew there was more to the story than what she'd been told. She had to find out the truth, no matter what it took.

"I can't let it go," Morgan said, her voice low and firm. "Not until I know the truth. Not until I know what really happened that night."

Mueller leaned forward, his hands clasped together on his desk. "Then consider this a warning, Cross. You're on thin ice. One wrong move and I'll have to report it to the higher-ups."

Morgan stood up, feeling tense and frustrated. She couldn't resist a biting comment: "The higher-ups? They've already taken my side once, Mueller."

His eyes flashed, and she almost regretted making it personal. But Mueller said, "It's true that Deputy Director Irvin overrode my conditions for your return, but I can respect the chain of command. He had his reasons for wanting you back, but he won't be there to hold your hand through everything, Cross, and if I send this to him, he might not like it, either."

Morgan bit her tongue. She didn't like the idea of Irvin thinking less of her when he'd given her a chance.

"I understand, sir," she said. "And I'll be careful."

She left Mueller's office, her mind racing. What was she going to do now? She couldn't give up on her investigation, but she also couldn't risk her job or her freedom. She needed a plan.

She also needed to know who the hell took those photos.

Was it another agent? Someone Mueller sent after her? Had someone been following her this whole time?

Or could it have even been Derik?

She hated to admit it, but it wasn't completely out of reach. The thought made Morgan's blood burn. Derik had been treating her with kid gloves lately, patronizing her at times. Maybe he didn't believe in her as much as he'd let on, and now, the mask was coming off.

If he was responsible for this, she needed to know.

Morgan decided to confront Derik about the pictures. She found him in the break room, sipping on a cup of coffee. When he saw her, he put his cup down and stood up, a look of concern on his face.

"Is everything okay?" he asked.

Morgan narrowed her eyes at him. "Did you take those pictures of me and Clancy Smith?"

Derik's expression shifted from concerned to defensive. "What are you talking about? What pictures?"

"The ones that were on Mueller's computer," Morgan said. "The ones of me with Clancy Smith."

Derik shook his head. "I don't know what you're talking about. I haven't seen any pictures."

She clenched her teeth, unsure if she believed him. After all, Derik had given up on her at some point, under his own admission.

Maybe he'd lost faith in her, too, but he had just left that part out.

Or maybe Mueller had something on him and was having him tail her. Derik knew her best in the FBI; he could know how to follow her without getting caught.

Derik's eyes narrowed. "What are you accusing me of, Morgan? You think I'm involved in some kind of conspiracy against you?"

"All I know is that someone's been following me, taking pictures of me," she said.

"And you think it was me?" Derik's face fell, like he was genuinely hurt, and it was enough to make Morgan second-guess herself. She had no proof it was Derik. She was just angry and lashing out at the world, and she didn't like the way Derik had been treating her lately. The “conditions” of their partnership. The way he’d been acting like she was a loose cannon, always in need of supervision.

"So, you're saying it wasn't?" Morgan asked.

"No," Derik said, "it wasn't me, Cross. I don't know who it was."

Morgan turned away. The last thing she needed was another unknown enemy, lurking in the shadows and following her. She couldn't let this pass.

"Cross," Derik said, "you've spent too long chasing shadows and watching behind your back. Now, you think even the people who care about you are your enemy."

Morgan couldn't look at him. Emotion welled inside her chest. Derik was saying he cared about her, even if he did reject her advance before. She wanted to believe in him, but she felt so wounded. Wounded by everything.

"Yeah, well, that's what ten years in prison will get you," she muttered.

"I'm sorry, Morgan." Derik's eyes were earnest. Sincere. "I know what you went through was awful. I know you lost so much. But I'm not the enemy here."

Morgan nodded slowly, still not looking at him. But he was getting through to her. Derik, of all people, should be the one person she could trust.

And yet she still couldn’t, with one hundred percent certainty, say she did trust him.

But he was still her friend, and her partner, and she had no proof it *was* him, either.

"I know," she said. "I'm sorry too. I'm just ... I'm so frustrated. I feel like I'm hitting a wall at every turn."

"It's understandable," Derik said. "But you can't let it consume you. You have to take care of yourself."

Morgan finally looked at him. "What do you mean?"

"I mean," Derik said, "that you need to be careful. You can't go off half-cocked, chasing leads that might not even pan out. You have a lot to lose, Morgan. Your freedom, your job ..."

"I know that," Morgan said, frustration creeping back into her voice. "I'm not stupid, Derik. I'm just trying to find the truth. I feel like I can’t trust anyone. Not even you.”

"I know," Derik said. "But you have to be smart about it. You have to think things through, and you have to be careful who you trust."

Morgan nodded slowly. "I know," she said. "You're right."

Derik reached out and put a hand on her shoulder. "I'm here for you, Morgan," he said. "If you need anything, just let me know. I know building trust with me, and everyone else out here, is gonna take time. I get it, really, I do."

Morgan felt a warmth spread through her chest. She was glad not all had changed between them. "Thanks, Derik. Sorry, again."

"Don't worry about it." He smiled, pulling his hand away.

"Who do you think it was?" Morgan asked, not expecting a real answer.

"I don't know," Derik said, "but maybe be more careful when you use the FBI database. C'mon, let's get back to work."

He left the room, but what he'd said stuck to her mind like glue. She wasn't sure why, but something about it got her mind turning back to the case. The database. There could be more information on Jerry Jameson that she'd missed, or on his business, something that could get them closer to the truth. She wasn't sure if Jerry was truly the guy they were looking for.

And if the killer was still out there, then the risks were too high to stop looking.

CHAPTER TWENTY

Hunched over her computer in her office, Morgan skimmed through Jerry's company's financial records. There wasn't much to see, considering he mostly got paid in cash. What he did have was just enough to make his business legitimate, but Morgan could tell by the client list that he had a lot more than he let off.

The company had a website, and Morgan checked its login records. Most of the logins traced back to Jerry's sister's house, the IP matching up with the location she'd found him at earlier. But there were a few strange logins from places all over the city. Morgan typed the IPs in, and they showed locations on the city map. Some were from neighborhoods close to where the victims lived. Maybe he had assistants.

But when Morgan checked more into the IPs, she noted that one was at a public library. Another, an internet café. She frowned, leaning back in her chair as she read over the information. If Jerry had assistants, then why would they be logging in from public spaces?

She'd just have to go ask him herself. They were keeping him in the interrogation room for now until they figured out what to do with him. There was a lot of paperwork to be done, but they had a strong enough case to keep Jerry in custody.

Morgan stood up from her chair, grabbing her badge and gun on her way out. She walked down the hallway and toward the interrogation room, her mind swimming with possibilities. If Jerry was innocent, then who was the killer? Could it really be Johnson?

Morgan shook her head, trying to clear her thoughts. She couldn't jump to conclusions. She needed to talk to Jerry first.

When she arrived at the interrogation room, she found Jerry sitting at the table, his hands cuffed in front of him. He looked up as she entered, his eyes flickering with recognition.

"Agent Cross," he said, his voice low and hoarse.

Morgan took a seat across from him. "Mr. Jameson," she said. "I need to ask you some questions."

Jerry sighed, leaning back in his chair. "I've been through this before," he said. "I don't know anything about those girls."

"I'm not here to talk about them," Morgan said. "I want to talk about your business."

"What about it?" Jerry asked, his eyes narrowing.

Morgan leaned forward, her voice low. "I know you have more clients than what's listed on your bank statements," she said.

Jerry's eyes widened in surprise, but he quickly regained his composure. "I don't see how that's your business, Agent Cross."

Morgan leaned back in her chair, studying him. "It's my business because those clients could be linked to the murders."

Jerry scoffed. "I don't have anything to do with those girls' deaths. I already told you that."

Morgan wasn't so sure. "Then why the secret clients?"

He sighed. "Look, I just ... it's not that big of a deal, okay? I do a bit of tax evasion. The super rich of this country do it all the time, but a little independent business like me gets hammered for it? How is that fair?"

"I don't care about your business practices, Mr. Jameson," Morgan said. "All I care about is finding out who killed those girls."

Jerry's eyes flashed. "You don't think it was me anymore?"

"It could be you," Morgan said. "It might not be. I noticed several strange logins to your company site. Do you have assistants or employees who may have logged in?"

Jerry's brows pinched. "No assistants, no ... I do most of the work myself, saves me some money. I do have a couple guys on my payroll, but one of 'em just quit, the other's my buddy, but he's on vacation, so it's just been me making house calls."

"Then who could have logged into your website?"

"I've never given anyone the passwords. I deal with all that stuff myself."

Morgan's brows pinched. "Did you login from any libraries? An internet café?"

"No ..." Jerry frowned. "I've only ever logged in from my sister's. That's where I conduct most of my clerical work."

Morgan's gut twisted with suspicion. Jerry was lying, she could feel it. "Are you sure about that?" she asked.

"Positive," Jerry said.

Morgan leaned across the table. "Because I have the IP addresses of logins from public spaces, Jerry. Someone has been logging in to your company website from public locations all over the city."

Jerry clenched his jaw. "I don't know anything about that," he said.

Morgan leaned back in her chair, studying him. There was a chance he was telling the truth, but she couldn't risk it. She needed to follow up on those IP addresses, find out who had been logging in from public spaces. Was it possible he'd been hacked?

Just then, Morgan's phone rang. She pulled it out to see Derik's name on her screen. She looked up at Jerry, then nodded and slipped out of the room. Once in the hall, she answered right away.

"Greene, what's going on?"

"Cross, George Johnson tried to skip town," Derik said. "We've got him in custody."

Morgan's heart sunk. She had been so focused on Jerry and their suspicions about his business that she had almost forgotten about Johnson. "What do you mean, he tried to skip town?"

"He was at the airport, trying to board a flight out of the country," Derik said. "We caught him just in time. He's in custody now."

Morgan felt a rush of relief. If Johnson was the killer, then they had caught him before he could get away. "Good work, Derik. I'm coming right now."

***

Once again, Morgan found herself face-to-face with George Johnson, alone in an interrogation room. This time, he was sweatier, more agitated than the first time. And this time, she wouldn't be so willing to let him off the hook.

"Where were you going, George?" Morgan asked. "Convenient time for a vacation, don't you think?"

He glowered at her. "This is nonsense. You let me go in exchange for my information, so I'm free to go wherever I please."

"Except your information is bullshit," Morgan fired back. "Jerry Jameson claimed he was never experimenting with the Bleeding Woodbine or any poisonous plants."

"Of course, he's gonna deny it," George said.

The problem was that Morgan believed Jerry more than she believed George. It was just her gut feelings talking, but still. George was the dirty one, and Jerry had been far more cooperative. That didn't mean he was innocent, of course, but Morgan wasn't done with George.

"Are you sure about that?" Morgan asked, leaning forward. "Because I have reason to believe that someone else may have been logging in to his company website from public spaces."

George's eyes widened for a moment before he quickly regained his composure. "I don't know what you're talking about."

Morgan leaned back in her chair, studying George. "I think you do," she said. "I think you've been trying to frame Jerry this whole time."

George's expression was unreadable. "And why would I do that?"

"So, you can keep getting away with your twisted game."

George laughed. "You're wasting time with me, Special Agent Cross. Jerry is the man you want. I'm telling you, he experimented with the Bleeding Woodbine in my class. Him and that stupid friend of his."

"What friend?" Morgan asked, frowning.

Suddenly, George's eyebrows pinched together, and his eyes darted around, as if he were remembering something. "I guess I didn't mention that," he said. "Jerry had a friend in class. Another troublemaker. Randall-something-or-other. Fink, I think his last name was. I can't remember."

Morgan frowned. Randall. Jerry mentioned that he had a friend on his payroll. A friend who would know him well, who might be able to figure out his password to log in to his site, maybe to get personal information on clients. Jerry had said his "buddy" was on vacation. But maybe Randall never went on vacation at all.

Morgan needed to know more. George was no reliable source of information, that was for sure. She needed to hear it from Jerry.

Morgan left the interrogation room, her mind racing with possibilities. She needed to talk to Jerry again, confront him with this new information. She found Jerry in the same room she had left him in, sitting quietly in his chair, lost in thought.

"Jerry, I need to ask you about your friend, Randall Fink," Morgan said as she walked in.

Jerry looked up, surprised. "Randall? What about him?"

"Is he the one who works with you?"

"Yes ..." Jerry blinked, confused.

"Did he experiment with the Bleeding Woodbine when you were in school together?" she asked, her heart in her throat. "Is that why the professor thought you did too?"

"I can't remember," Jerry admitted. "I was drunk and high for most of university, I really didn't get far."

"You mentioned that he was on vacation, but I have reason to believe that he's been logging in to your company website from public spaces," Morgan said. "Maybe to get information on your clients, the ones you didn't share with him."

Jerry's face contorted with anger. "No way. Randall would never do something like that. He's my friend, my business partner. He's been with me since the beginning."

"But do you trust him?" Morgan asked, keeping her voice level.

Jerry hesitated, his eyes flickering with uncertainty. "I mean, yeah, of course I trust him. He's my friend. Besides, he's in Hawaii."

"How sure are you that he's on vacation?" Morgan asked. "Did he send you any photos?"

"No, but ..." Jerry shook his head. "Look, it's not Randy. His aunt just died about a month ago, so he went on vacation to Hawaii to clear his head. His aunt practically raised him. I haven't even seen the guy since."

The story was building in Morgan's head rapidly, the pieces clicking in place. This aunt of Randall's dying could be what had triggered this string of murders. And Randall had conveniently gone off the map since.

But the real question was whether he was truly in Hawaii or not. If he were, then he was innocent.

Morgan zipped out of the room, leaving Jerry in a confused panic. She dashed back to her office and went on the computer, pulling up Randall Fink's information. If he'd taken a flight, it would be recorded. He'd have bought a ticket. There'd be a record of his travel, a paper trail.

But there was no record of Randall's flight to Hawaii. In fact, he hadn't purchased anything at all since before the murders. It told Morgan nothing, other than that he'd gone off the grid. She leaned back in her chair, frustrated.

Randall had gone off the map. He'd disappeared like smoke in the wind. But why? What could he be hiding? Morgan felt a chill run down her spine as she considered all the possibilities, but they only made her more determined to find out who Randall Fink really was.

She went into the FBI database. Randall's driver's license photo showed a gaunt man with pock marks on his cheeks and soulless eyes. His parents were deceased, apparently, but he'd lived with his aunt, Tilly.

Morgan opened up Tilly's file.

And there, staring back at her, was a photo of a red-haired woman.

CHAPTER TWENTY ONE

Morgan's car whipped up to the curb. The old, abandoned-looking house was surrounded by overgrown grass, the paint peeling on its crumbling walls. The windows were shuttered, and an eerie silence hung in the air. An old, rusty gate creaked in the wind, and the front porch sagged dangerously to one side. The house seemed out of place against the otherwise lively street. The late-afternoon sky had darkened, threatening more rain.

Eyeing the place, Morgan took out her phone and tried Derik again. He hadn't been picking up, and she wasn't sure what had him so tied down, but he was MIA. And Morgan couldn't wait, not for a team, not for anything.

She had to follow her gut on this. And her gut led her here.

If she were wrong, then she could accept that. But she needed to know more about Randall, to find out if he was here. This was the house he had lived in with his aunt before she died. Randall never moved out, never had a wife, a girlfriend, nothing. He just worked as a gardener and lived with his aunt. Very odd, for a man pushing forty.

As disheveled as the house was, the garden out front was pristine. Well-taken care of. And recently.

Morgan tried Derik again, but was sent to voicemail.

"Damn it, Greene," she muttered, then sent him a text:

Tried to call you. I'm doing things my way.

Then she sent him the address and turned her phone on silent. If Derik showed up, then great. But Morgan wasn't going to wait around. There was no time, not if Randall was truly the killer.

She got out of her car and walked toward the house. The gate squeaked louder as she pushed it open, and she made her way up the porch steps. The wood creaked under her feet, and she held her breath as she knocked on the door.

There was no answer.

Morgan tried the handle, and to her surprise, it turned. She pushed the door open slowly and stepped inside. The air was musty, and the room was dimly lit.

Morgan took out her flashlight and shone it around the room. The furniture was covered in white sheets, and the only thing that seemed to be in use was a desk in the corner. Papers, folders, and photos were scattered all over it. Morgan walked over to it and started to sift through them.

The first photo she found was of a young Randall Fink with his arm around a red-haired woman. The woman in the photo was the same woman in Tilly's file. Morgan's heart began to race as she realized the woman was Randall's aunt.

The documents were all in order, but there was something off about them. Morgan couldn't put her finger on it.

She turned her attention toward the living room, where more photos of Randall and Tilly were hanging on the walls, some of them showing the progression of his life—and hers. Tilly had died of natural causes, it said, and by the time she'd passed, her hair had gone from red to gray. And yet the women being murdered had vibrant red hair, like the photos of Tilly that hung around the house.

Perhaps this was the version Randall had fantasized about killing, over and over again, until he started taking real women.

But where was Randall now? Morgan's heart was pounding as she tried to piece together the puzzle. She moved toward the kitchen but stopped short when she felt her phone vibrate. Derik was calling.

She answered and quietly said, "Greene—"

"Cross, sorry I missed you," he said. "Tell me you're not at that address."

"I am," Morgan said. "Where've you been?"

"Mueller has Johnson working on that antidote he wrote a paper on," Derik explained. "In exchange for his freedom, of course, but we're not gonna give it to him unless we figure out if he's really innocent."

"He might be," Morgan said. "Derik, you need to get here. Now."

"I'm on my way."

Morgan hung up and continued through the kitchen, her flashlight illuminating the old, rusty appliances. She wondered if Randall had ever used any of them, or if he had just eaten out every night. In the back of the kitchen, she found a door to the basement.

The stairs creaked under her feet as she descended into the darkness. She shone her flashlight around, her heart beating in her chest. The basement was empty, save for a few boxes. She navigated her way back upstairs, but there was no sign of life in this house. Nothing at all. It seemed even the spiders had died in the absence of Tilly.

Going back upstairs, Morgan made her way across the living room, her feet creaking on the old wood floors. No one was here. And there was no evidence Randall was truly the killer, other than these creepy photos of his aunt who happened to look a lot like the victims did.

Morgan sighed, worried she was just wasting more time. All of these family photos, as unnerving as they were, reminded her of her father. The only person to visit her often and consistently in prison, until he'd died before she was even out.

She never got to go to his funeral.

Hadn't visited his tombstone yet. She couldn't bring herself to do it.

She'd missed so much of her father's life, but his faith in her had never wavered. He'd always known she was innocent. She'd never forget the kindness he'd shown her, the only light she had in an otherwise dark world. Prison had been her personal hell, but her dad had still been there for her, as he had been her whole life.

Morgan slowly made her way back to the living room and studied another portrait of Randall Fink with Tilly. They looked stiff, unhappy. Nothing like the photos Morgan had with her father. She'd always felt at ease around him, and she missed him more than words could describe.

She missed his voice, his laughter. She missed having dinner at his house before she went to prison. She missed his sense of humor and his easygoing nature. She missed the way he'd make her feel safe and protected, no matter what was happening in the world around her. She missed his hugs, his warmth, and his unconditional love.

Life felt so cold without him. Cold and empty. All Morgan could do was stand there in silence, thinking about all of the moments she'd missed with her father and how much she wished he was still here.

Then she heard a noise.

A creaking. Morgan whipped around, only to see the front door slowly being pushed open.

Morgan placed her hand on her gun, ready for anything.

CHAPTER TWENTY TWO

When Sarah woke up, she couldn't move her legs.

It took her a moment to orient herself, to understand why she felt so constricted. What had happened? Last thing she knew, she had been going into her kitchen while the gardener had worked outside, and now, it was much later in the day, nearly evening, judging by the sky. And the back of her skull throbbed with pain.

Sarah tried to move, and that was when she realized it: she was surrounded by dirt, half-buried. She looked down and saw grass up to her chest, all around her, partially burying her alive. For a moment, she was sure it was a nightmare. But she didn't wake up.

"Help!" she called out. She looked around, only to realize there were hedges on either side of her.

Hedges ...

Like she was in a maze.

Sarah's blood ran cold as the reality settled onto her. The Maze Killer. She'd heard about it on the news. But what had happened to her gardener? The man Jerry sent? He was—

No. It hit her like a brick.

The Maze Killer was the gardener. The very man she had let into her home.

Sarah felt a cold sweat break out on her forehead as she struggled to free herself from the dirt and the grass. She had to get out of there. She had to find a way out of the maze before the killer came back for her. But no matter how hard she pushed, she couldn't break free. The soil wrapped around her like a strong snake, never letting go. Fear flooded her. Could this really be the end?

But then something stirred within her. Determination. She would not go down without a fight. Renewed energy surged through her, and she kept trying. She made some progress, wriggling her toes and pushing against the grass and soil with all her strength. But the dirt seemed determined to keep her in its clutches, like some dark force had taken residence in the maze walls—one that was eager to keep Sarah from escaping.

It felt like no matter how much she pushed and clawed at the dirt around her, it just kept coming back stronger than ever before, trapping her even further in its grasp.

And then she heard a sound, a rustling in the bushes. Footsteps, coming closer.

Sarah froze, her heart pounding in her chest. It was the Maze Killer, coming to finish her off. It had to be.

Sarah's heart raced, and she clawed at the dirt with all her strength—but still, no matter how hard she tried, she couldn't seem to get free. The sound grew closer and closer, until Sarah was sure he would find her any moment now. She dug and clawed with all her might, tears streaming down her face as she prayed for a miracle—and yet, try as she might, the grass held tight around her limbs, firmly in place like an iron vice.

Then the footsteps were right in front of her.

Petrified, she dared to look up.

And there he was. The gardener. He had an eerie smile on his face, and he was holding fresh flowers in his arms.

"Ah, you're awake," he said. "You look marvelous."

"L-let me go!" she exclaimed.

"Oh, my dear," he said, "it's already too late for you. The poison is inside you, making its way through your system ... but they won't know that." He draped a flower over her shoulder.

"Who?" Sarah asked. This guy was insane. She just had to keep talking, maybe see if she could somehow get through to him. "Please, I-I have a life, sir. My parents will be devastated. My mom just lost her sister, and she—"

"You lost your aunt?" he cut in.

Sarah flinched, taken aback. "Yes ..."

He pouted, then draped another flower over her shoulder. "So sad for you. That's okay. Your life will be somcthing beautiful. Every garden needs its centerpiece."

Sarah's eyes widened in terror as she realized what he meant. He was going to make her a part of his sick garden. The Maze Killer had struck again.

She opened her mouth to scream, but the poison made her throat constrict, taking away her voice. She was trapped, unable to move, unable to escape. Her eyes flickered to the man holding the flowers, and she saw the madness in his eyes. He was enjoying this.

Sarah closed her eyes and prayed for a miracle. She had always been a fighter, but now, she was powerless. The poison worked its way through her veins, making her feel weak and dizzy. She knew she didn't have much time left.

Sarah shuddered, terror gripping her insides. She knew she had to do something, anything, to get away from this man. But she was so weak, so trapped in the dirt around her. She couldn't even move her legs. She had to keep trying, keep fighting.

"Please," she begged, "you don't have to do this. I won't tell anyone, I swear. Just let me go. Please."

The man laughed, and it sent shivers down Sarah's spine. "Oh, my dear. You don't understand. This is what I have to do. It's what I was meant to do. I'm a gardener, you know. And every garden needs its flowers. You'll be perfect."

Sarah's heart felt like it was going to stop. She had to think, had to come up with a plan. But her mind was foggy, her thoughts jumbled. She couldn't focus.

"Please, I'm a person," she said. "A person, just like you. I have a life. Hopes. Dreams. Please ..."

"I'm so sorry, dear," he said. *"She* never showed me any mercy. *She* never cared about my pain. And you, dear Sarah, are just like her."

"Like who?" Sarah felt tears wet her cheeks. "Who are you talking about? I'm not her! I've never hurt you!"

The gardener's smile shifted to a sneer. "Oh, but you have. You've hurt me just like she did. You've hurt me by existing, by taking up space in this world that she no longer can. And now, you'll be a part of my garden, just like she is."

Sarah's mind raced. Who was this woman he was talking about? And how could she use that to her advantage?

"Please, tell me who she is," Sarah said. "Maybe I can help you. Maybe we can find a way to honor her memory, rather than destroy more lives."

The gardener's expression softened, and he looked thoughtful for a moment. "You know, you're not like her at all. She was cruel. She never cared about anyone but herself. But you ... you have a kind heart. It's too bad about that hair of yours."

"My hair?" Sarah looked at her orange hair, draping over the dirt.

"I think I'll take a piece of it," he said, "to remember you by." He took out scissors, and they gleamed in the light. He grabbed a piece of her hair and snipped it off, marveling at it, before he looked down at her with a twisted smile.

"Don't worry, dear," he said. "It will all be over soon."

Sarah could feel herself fading. The last thing she saw was the gardener's calm, smiling face before she faded into the black.

CHAPTER TWENTY THREE

Morgan held her gun up toward the door of the house, ready to shoot if she had to. Randall could be behind that door, ready to jump at her, but she wouldn't let that happen.

He was the killer. She was sure of it.

The door creaked open more. Morgan bit her lip, eyeing down her sights.

Then the door fully opened.

But it wasn't Randall on the other side. A short, old woman with a gray perm and a floral dress stood on the other side, holding up a dish full of food. The woman's eyes widened at what she saw, and the casserole dish fell to the floor, exploding into a gooey mess.

"O-oh my!"

Morgan lowered her gun immediately and held up her hands to show the woman she meant no harm. "Ma'am, I'm so sorry," Morgan said, quickly flashing her FBI badge. The old woman scowled at her, clearly still recovering from the shock.

"Who are you?" she croaked out. "What are you doing in Randy's house?"

Morgan put her gun back in its holster, her heart calming. It was just his neighbor, delivering him some food, it seemed. "You know the man who lives here?" Morgan asked.

"Of course, I was just coming by to drop off his dinner, the poor thing," she said. "I'm his neighbor, Joan. You're with the FBI?"

"I am," Morgan said. "I'm sorry I scared you."

Joan looked down at her dish and sighed. "These things happen, I suppose ... where is Randy?"

"I'm looking for him," Morgan said. "He's wanted in connection to an important case."

"Is he in trouble?"

Morgan swallowed. This old lady seemed nice, innocent, like she had no idea Randall was almost certainly the Maze Killer.

"I just need to find him," Morgan said.

"He lost his aunt, the poor boy," she said, looking around the room. "He's a lovely young man, helps me with my garden free of charge. He's not in trouble with the police, is he?"

Morgan didn't have time for this. She ushered the woman out of the house, leaving the mess of food on the floor. They went outside, and Morgan shut the door behind her.

"Please, go back to your house, ma'am," Morgan said. "I'll take it from here."

Joan looked at her with a sad expression. "I hope Randy is okay. He's been through so much already."

Morgan couldn't help but feel a twinge of guilt. This old woman had no idea what her neighbor was capable of. She couldn't let her guard down around anyone, not even a sweet, old lady like Joan.

"I'll make sure he's okay," Morgan said, trying to sound reassuring. "Thank you for your help."

Joan nodded and shuffled away, leaving Morgan alone on the sidewalk. She looked up and down the street, trying to decide where to go next. She knew she had to find Randall, but where could he be? And where was Derik?

Morgan took out her phone and quickly called Mueller—he was likely still at HQ, and he could give her an update on what was going on with all the mazes in the city. The police and FBI were watching all of them, but maybe there was one they missed. Mueller picked up within a few rings.

"Cross, what's going on?"

"Mueller, I need your help," Morgan said. "What's going on with the mazes? Has anyone seen anything?"

"No, but we've got Johnson making up that antidote," he said. "It might not work, but it's the best thing we've got."

"Good, but we need to know where he's going to strike next. Is it possible we missed any locations in the city?" Morgan pulled up a map on her phone, keeping Mueller on speaker, and her GPS zeroed in on her current location.

"I don't know, Cross, we've got all hands on deck."

She zoomed out slightly, and that was when she saw it: located nearby, on the outskirts of town, was an old cornfield.

A cornfield with a maze.

Not only that, but as Morgan took in the aerial view of it, something stood out. It was outside of town, near a forest with a river running through it. And the name of the river?

Doe River.

Little Doe.

The riddle … was it really this all along?

"What about the corn maze on the northern outskirts of town?" Morgan asked. "There's a river near it called Doe River. That could be a reference to the note we received from the killer."

Mueller went quiet for a moment. Then, he said, "It's not on our radar. We considered it out of bounds."

"Sir," Morgan said, heart in her throat, "if this Randall Fink is our guy, then that maze—it's right near his house."

Mueller cursed under his breath. "We've got teams searching all the other mazes. But I'll send a team to check it out."

"I'm heading there now," Morgan said firmly. "I'm not waiting for backup."

"Cross, you can't go in there alone," Mueller protested.

"I don't have a choice," Morgan said, her voice hard. "I'll call you with updates."

She hung up and took off running toward her car. She had to get to that corn maze, fast. She could feel her heart racing and her breath coming in quick gasps. She might be walking into a trap, but she had to take the risk. This was her job, and she was damn good at it.

She peeled out of the driveway and took off down the road toward the maze, the tires screeching as she slammed on the gas.

***

The traffic wouldn't let up as Derik made his way toward the outskirts of town, ripping up to the house Morgan had told him to go to. The old building had seen better days, which was the first thing he noticed.

The second was that Morgan's car wasn't there.

Frowning, he took out his phone and tried to call her, but she didn't pick up. Derik had a bad feeling inside him. Morgan had specifically given him this address, so where was she?

She was bolder, more reckless since she was released from prison, and part of him was terrified she'd do something even more reckless and get herself hurt. She'd already gotten shot in the leg the other day.

As Derik approached the house, he noticed it was quiet. Too quiet. He unsheathed his gun and cautiously made his way to the front door, which was slightly ajar. On the floor was a pool of food next to a casserole dish. What the hell happened here? Pushing it open, he stepped inside the dimly lit living room.

"Morgan?" he called out, his heart pounding in his chest.

No response.

He made his way through the house, checking each room as he went. It was silent, except for the creaking of the old house settling. Creepy photos of Randall and his dead aunt lined the walls, sending a chill up Derik's spine. But there was no sign of Morgan anywhere in this house.

Stepping over the food, he went back outside as a gust of wind burst through the air.

Derik jolted when he noticed a woman standing on the sidewalk, staring at him like something out of a horror movie.

"Are you looking for that woman?" the old woman asked.

Realizing she was just an old lady, not a threat, Derik cautiously approached her. "Yes, ma'am. She was here?"

"She was," the woman said. "She was looking for Randall here. She told me to go inside, then I saw her speed off in a hurry in her car."

Derik's heart sank. Morgan had gone off to find Randall alone, without waiting for backup. She was putting herself in danger, and in Derik's gut, he knew he had to find her before it was too late. He thanked the old woman and took off running toward his car, his mind racing with different scenarios of what could have happened to Morgan.

The first thing he did was call Mueller, who picked up within a few rings. "Greene—"

"Where's Cross?" Derik cut in.

"She went to some corn maze on the northern outskirts," Mueller said. "We're sending backup."

"She's not answering her phone. I'm close by now."

"Then you'd better get there, Greene, before Cross gets herself hurt. The team is on their way."

Derik hung up. He couldn't bear the thought of Morgan getting herself killed over something so reckless. As he drove toward the outskirts of town, he tried calling Morgan again. Still no answer. As Derik sped down the road toward the corn maze, his mind was racing. He couldn't shake the feeling that something was wrong. Morgan was a skilled FBI agent, but she had a tendency to be reckless, especially when it came to catching a criminal. He wasn't sure why he was suddenly so worried about her, but it caused him to press harder on the gas, hurling himself forward on the long backroad.

Just then, a deer jumped out of the darkness in front of Derik's car. He swerved to dodge it, but it was too late. His car slid off the road. He was hurling uncontrollably toward a pole, so he had to swerve.

He heard a loud thump. Derik suddenly realized he wasn't in control anymore. Everything around him was a blur. He felt himself spinning, trying to break away from a force that was much greater than himself. His car had been hit by a truck going the opposite direction, and he could feel his car flipping through the air, spinning out of control before finally slamming down hard on its side on the road. The last thing Derik saw were two bright headlights coming straight for him as he lost consciousness ...

CHAPTER TWENTY FOUR

Tall stalks of corn surrounded Morgan on all sides.

The sun had set, leaving a darkness in the sky that chilled her to the bone as she hurried through the corn maze, aimless, yet focused. If the Maze Killer was here—if he had another victim—then she would find him. Despite the discomfort and pain from her leg wound, Morgan kept running. Her limp was pronounced, and her stride had become uneven as she forced her body forward, determined to find the killer and any potential victims. She gritted her teeth against the pain, feeling a sharp jolt in her leg with each step she took.

The light of the full moon illuminated the tall stalks of dried corn, creating shadows that danced in and out of the maze as Morgan rushed through.

As she turned a corner, Morgan heard a muffled sound. She paused, listening intently. It was coming from up ahead. She made her way through the stalks, remaining as quiet as possible. The sound grew louder as she neared, and she could make out a voice—a man's voice—speaking in hushed tones.

Morgan raised her gun, inching forward slowly. She could hear the sound of a man talking, and she knew she was getting closer.

"My precious flower," the man's voice said. "It will all be over soon."

Morgan went to dash forward, but pain shot up her leg from the wound, causing her to buckle. It seemed a stitch had ripped out, probably from all the running and stress she'd put on her body. The man's voice went quiet, and Morgan stopped breathing so she could hear every sound around her.

But there were no sounds.

Only the rustling of corn stalks in the breeze.

Still, she knew what she'd done. She'd alerted him.

He knew she was here.

Morgan stood on shaky legs, still holding her gun, determined to see this through. Even if it killed her. What else did she have to live for?

She had been in prison for years, and even after her release, she couldn't leave the past behind. This case had become everything to her, and she wouldn't rest until she had caught the Maze Killer. She knew she was risking her life, but she had nothing else to lose.

As she moved forward, she saw a figure up ahead between the stalks. She aimed her gun, ready to shoot. Until she got closer and caught a glimmer of red hair in the moonlight.

It was a victim. A woman, half-buried in the dirt, adorned with flowers. Morgan didn't think—she just ran forward, tucking her gun away as she landed on her knees, ignoring the pain. The woman was unconscious, but Morgan stuck her fingers to her throat. She had warmth. A pulse.

Life.

It wasn't too late.

The hope flooded Morgan enough to drown her. She reached for her phone in her pocket when, suddenly, a sharp pain jabbed through her arm.

Morgan looked beside her in horror to see a man, wearing overalls, holding up a needle with a wicked smile. She went for her gun, but he dashed through the maze before she could even react.

She couldn't think about the pain in her arm, about the strangely warm feeling that now seeped into her veins. The poison she knew she'd just been injected with.

No.

She had to catch him.

Morgan stood up, taking out her gun, and chased the Maze Killer into the unknown.

The pain in Morgan's leg was nothing compared to the fear and adrenaline coursing through her body. She knew she had to find the Maze Killer before the poison took its toll. She stumbled through the maze, her eyes darting left and right, her senses heightened. She could hear the sound of footsteps growing fainter by the second. She knew she was getting closer.

The poison worked fast, and Morgan could feel her body weakening by the second. She stumbled through the maze, her vision blurring as she tried to keep up with the man. Her gun felt heavy in her hand, and she knew she didn't have long before she would lose consciousness.

As she turned a corner, she saw a figure up ahead. It was the man, standing with his back to her. Morgan raised her gun, aiming for his head.

"Freeze!" she yelled, but the man didn't move.

"Put your hands up!" she yelled, her voice echoing through the maze.

The Maze Killer slowly turned his head, revealing a face that was unremarkable in every way. Morgan expected him to look more sinister, more terrifying. But he just looked like an ordinary man.

"I've been expecting you, Agent Cross," he said, his voice deep and smooth. "I must admit that I'm impressed. You've come farther than I thought you would."

Morgan kept her gun steady, her breathing ragged. But she found that the gun was weighing more by the second, and she could barely hold it up. Even if she did shoot, she doubted it would be in a straight line, and Randall, the killer, seemed to know that.

He turned to her with a calm smile.

"I'm impressed," he said. "I wanted someone to find me, and the police simply weren't enough. But you were. You played well."

Morgan could feel herself fading. In her last moments, she found herself not thinking about her life, but wanting to know why he had done all of this. Why was she about to die? For what purpose?

What were the means to his ends?

"Tell me why," she croaked out, barely holding herself up. "Why did you do this? Why the notes?"

He walked closer to her. Morgan's finger went limp, and soon, the gun fell from her hands. She could barely hold her legs up, but she still could see him getting closer to her, blurring more and more by the second.

“It was all because of her,” he said.

“Your aunt,” Morgan said. At least she had learned some things on her own.

“That’s right,” he said. “She used to take me out here, you know. Leave me in here for hours. She’d write little notes, leave them as clues on how I could get out ..." He laughed, but it was full of angst. "I would cry and beg. I could never find my way out, no matter how many times she left me out here."

Morgan's vision was fading, but she held on, wanting to hear the rest of his story. It was a story that would never be heard by anyone else, and she wanted to know it all. If this was how she died, she could at least die understanding the sick mind of the person who killed her.

"So, you punished women who looked like her," Morgan said. "And you taunted us with your notes, the same way your aunt taunted you."

She collapsed to her knees. Almost over. She saw her dad's face, smiling. She'd be with him soon.

"That's right." The voice echoed around her. He was getting closer. "Smart and perceptive. You were worthy."

She didn't have much strength left. But she always kept a hunting knife strapped inside her boot. He got closer to her, and she could see his feet coming toward her face. She subtly reached for the knife. He was too busy talking to notice.

"My aunt was ... a cold woman," he said. "She could be lovely too. But mostly, she was cold. Vulgar ... I hated that red hair ... all my life ... then, by the time I finally got to see her die, all the red had faded. She'd become gray, a haggard, old bag. That was why I started to slip a little something extra into her evening teas."

"You killed her," Morgan said.

He was closer.

She gripped the knife.

"I did," he said, bemused. "But it didn't go how I'd always wanted. I craved more ... needed more. These young women had much redder hair. They were all like her."

His foot was right beside her now.

With the last bit of her strength, Morgan slashed forward. Her blade connected with his foot—snapping right into his Achilles's heel.

Randall yelped in pain and blood immediately poured from him. Morgan smiled to herself as she lay back on the grass. That wound would be awful. It might even kill him, she hoped. It would definitely slow him down. Derik would get him. He would pay for what he'd done.

She felt the poison slowing her body. Her eyes closed, and she stopped caring. There was no more. Her mind, her body, and her spirit were gone. But she looked forward to seeing her dad again.

Just then, she heard a voice. A familiar one. Morgan's eyes fluttered open a bit more to see the tips of the cornstalks and the night sky. But someone else too.

Derik.

His face appeared before hers. He had a wound on his head, bleeding down his pale skin, and a look of urgency in his eyes. He was shouting, but Morgan couldn't hear him anymore. She could only smile. At least she got to see him one last time.

Finally at peace, she let go of her final breath.

CHAPTER TWENTY FIVE

Morgan's eyes fluttered open to a white light.

For a moment, she wondered if Heaven were real. She'd blinked, died, then woke up here. It was a nice thought but too short-lived. A steady beeping slowly bled into her consciousness. She opened her eyes more and took in her mortal body, splayed out on the white sheets of a hospital bed, with IVs and tubes hooked up to her.

A hospital.

Of course.

Morgan wasn't sure why, for a moment, she was almost disappointed she didn't die. She had finally felt at peace, ready to let it all go. Her fight had been over.

And yet here she was, alive. Breathing.

And she wasn't alone.

"Cross, you're awake."

Derik's face was pale, with a look of intense emotion in his eyes—a mix of relief and sorrow. His forehead was bruised, and a white gauze was taped across it, holding it in place. His patched-up face stood out against the lightness of the room.

Morgan couldn't speak. She was overcome with emotions.

Derik had saved her life. He had risked everything to make sure she was okay. The thought made her heart swell with gratitude and affection for him. She tried to speak, but her throat was dry and sore. She cleared her throat and managed a faint whisper, "Thank you, Derik."

Derik's face softened, and he leaned in closer to her. "Are you kidding? I'm your partner. I'm just sorry I was late. Had a little car accident."

She wanted to cry, to scream, to hug him. But her body was still weak, and all she could do was look at him. The weight of everything that had happened crashed down on her. The Maze Killer, her own near-death experience, and now, the reality of surviving it all.

"How long have I been out?" she managed to croak out.

"A day," Derik replied. "You were pretty messed up, but you're getting better now. The nurses said your vitals were looking great."

Morgan looked down at herself. She was wearing a hospital gown, and she could feel the soreness in her body.

"What happened to Randall?" she asked.

"He's in custody," Derik said. "Thanks to you. You got him before he could get away."

Morgan smiled weakly. It was a relief to know he was behind bars, but it didn't take away the trauma of everything that had happened. Her mind was still spinning with questions.

"But ... the poison," Morgan said.

"Johnson's experimental antidote worked. He's been working on it for years, but it wasn't perfected, as he never got to trial it on humans. But it was the best we had, so we tried it out. Both you and Sarah are going to be okay."

Morgan wanted to cry but held it all in. Suddenly, she was ashamed of the thought she'd had—that it would have been better to just die. How had she lost herself like that? How had she given up on herself? She was grateful Derik couldn't see inside her mind.

Still, it made her laugh that Johnson, who she'd loathed the most throughout this case, had technically saved her life in the end.

"I'll be sure to send Johnson a postcard," Morgan muttered, and Derik laughed. "Why'd he try to run, anyway?"

"You're going to laugh, but apparently, he'd read up on your story and was paranoid he'd get framed too. I wouldn't have believed him before, but considering we know he's innocent now, I guess it checks out."

Derik was right; Morgan did laugh. "Well, getting framed for a crime you didn't commit is something you'd reasonably want to avoid. I can't blame him for that."

Derik laughed, too, his eyes lingering on hers. Silence spread between them for a moment, before Derik said, "You know, you're going to make it."

"I know," she said.

She was still in a lot of pain, but her arm and leg felt good enough to wiggle her fingers and toes. She was alive. It was a miracle. Her life had been saved, and she'd been brought back to the place she most wanted to be. She looked up at him and said, "It's you I'm thankful for."

Derik laughed. He touched her hand gently, and they both fell quiet. There was so much they wanted to say to each other, but they both knew it would have to wait. Something else was on Derik's mind too.

"I'm sorry I wasn't there sooner," he said. "I was ... when I crashed, I thought maybe we'd never see each other again."

"But we did," Morgan whispered.

For a long moment, they just stared at each other. Derik pulled his hand away, and Morgan missed the warmth of his fingertips on hers. He rubbed at his neck as he said, "Fink confessed to everything. His aunt took him in after his parents died, but I guess she was abusive."

"He told me," Morgan said. "I listened to his whole damn life story as the poison was killing me."

"That must've been terrifying."

"I was just happy I got a good hit on him."

"You sure did," Derik said. "He nearly bled out, but we resuscitated him. Now, he gets to rot in jail forever."

Jail. Morgan didn't want to think about that now, especially when she was trapped inside this hospital room. She hated the idea of not being able to walk free at any time she needed to. She'd endured too much of that already.

"Tell me I don't have to stay here long," Morgan said.

"No. We just have to keep an eye on you and let your body heal. They're releasing you tomorrow."

Morgan relaxed. Thank God.

They were quiet for a moment and then Derik smiled. "I guess you'll be glad to get out of here and get back on the street."

"You have no idea," Morgan said, and now, it was her turn to smile. "I know the FBI is risky, but I was made for this job, Greene. Same as you."

"It's in our blood, I guess," Derik said. "Mueller's impressed by you, as always. He'll be thrilled to hear you're awake."

"I'm just glad no one is telling me I'm a disappointment."

"Oh, they would never do that."

She and Derik shared a laugh.

"But seriously, I'm glad to see you back," Derik said, and his face shifted to a serious look. "I was afraid ... I'd lost you."

"Nope," Morgan said. "I'm damn hard to kill. Besides, I have to live with you now, remember?"

"Oh, shut up."

Derik rolled his eyes and laughed, and she knew everything would be okay. They went silent, listening only to the beeping on the monitor.

Morgan knew she owed Derik so much. If she'd been alone when the killer came after her, she wouldn't be sitting here right now. Or if she'd given in to the darkness, she would've never been able to fight her way back.

Derik had come for her. He had risked everything to save her. They were partners, sure, but he had cared about her. And she cared about him too.

But she knew, deep down, there was something else. Something she couldn't help but feel. She hadn't noticed it before, but with the soft light and the quiet, she could see the way his blue eyes shimmered.

She could feel the tension between them, the unspoken words, the raw emotions. She wanted to reach out and touch him, to feel the warmth of his skin against hers. But she didn't want to ruin their friendship, their partnership, with her feelings.

Derik cleared his throat, breaking the silence. "We should get some rest. I'll stay here with you, make sure you're okay."

Morgan nodded, grateful for his presence. She closed her eyes, feeling the weight of everything that had happened finally catch up to her. Derik's warmth was comforting, and she slowly drifted off to sleep, feeling safe for the first time in days.

EPILOGUE

Morgan relaxed on her couch, patting her dog's fur. A day after being released from the hospital, she was finally feeling like herself again. She'd decided to return home, just with extra security measures installed in case anyone wanted to leave her another flower.

She realized that it may have been Randall's handiwork anyway; he was the one obsessed with flowers, and he'd proven himself to be extremely sneaky and agile. He also said he knew who she was, so he'd been waiting for her, specifically, to come. She decided it was almost certainly him who'd left the flower. She'd interrogate him about it on another day, but until then, she needed to take it easy. Doctor's orders.

She sipped her cup of tea and sighed, wishing she could help but knowing the best thing she could do was to rest until she was fully recovered. She wanted a stiff drink but was taking a play from Derik's book tonight and laying off the booze.

Morgan melted into her couch, grateful to be here. She still felt shame for accepting her near-death. Her life was worth more than that. It had to be.

Suddenly, there was a knock at the door. She knew who it was—Derik. He'd asked to come over, so she shouted, "Come in!"

Derik poked his head in, his dark hair combed to the side. He smiled when he saw Morgan.

"Hey," he said. "How are you feeling?"

"Better," Morgan replied. "Thanks to you."

Derik walked over to the couch and sat down next to her. "I just wanted to check in on you, make sure you're doing okay."

"I am. And I owe you everything, you know."

Derik shook his head. "You don't owe me anything. We're partners, and I care about you."

Morgan smiled, feeling her heart flutter. She had to admit that she was starting to feel something more for Derik. She had been too scared to admit it before, but now that she had almost lost him, she realized how much she cared for him.

But before she could say anything, he said, "Hey, actually, there is one thing I'd ask of you."

"Anything," Morgan said.

"What's going on with the whole meeting a drug dealer thing?"

Morgan's heart sank. She didn't want to talk about that. But after Derik had come for her, it was the least she could do. Offer him up some truth. "Look," she said, "he was ... a connection I got from Samson."

"Samson?" Derik said, aghast. Of course, it sounded wrong that Morgan had listened to anything her mortal enemy had said.

But maybe Samson wasn't her ultimate enemy, after all. Maybe it was someone in the FBI, someone who had betrayed her that night. The thought made her head spin. She'd been a loyal agent before what happened, and she had no idea who had betrayed her.

"I know it's nuts," Morgan said, "but I heard there was someone there that night. A criminal, who called in the whole thing. That's who reported me."

Derik frowned. She knew she wasn't making any sense.

"I think it was an undercover agent, Derik," she said. "I think someone in the Bureau reported me, and that was why I wrongfully went to prison for ten damn years."

Derik was quiet, taking this all in. "And you got this information from ... Samson?"

"His connection told me more," Morgan said. "That Clancy person. That's why I was meeting him. I'm not some secret drug addict."

Derik laughed. "Well, I never thought that, but ..." He sighed. "Okay. I get why you'd want to do this, but can I ask one more thing? No more vigilante shit. If this is true, then I can help you, by the books. But no more secrets between us, Cross. If we're gonna keep being partners, that's what I need from you."

Morgan bit her lip. It was hard to open up to the world after what had happened to her. She was scared to trust, even Derik.

But maybe ... maybe it was the least she could do.

"Okay," she said.

Derik smiled. "Okay?"

"Yeah," Morgan said. "Let's do it together."

They fell into a comfortable silence, but Morgan felt at peace. And now that all that was out of the way, she felt emboldened to go on.

"Derik," she said, taking a deep breath. "I know we're partners, but ... there's something I need to tell you."

Derik looked at her, his eyes full of concern. "What is it?"

Morgan took another deep breath. "I think ... I think I'm starting to feel something more for you. I don't know if you feel the same way, but I just had to tell you. No secrets, right?"

Derik smiled softly. "Come on, Cross," he said. "You know I care about you too. But I think it might be best if we just stay professional. We still have to work together, and I don't want anything getting in the way of that."

Morgan nodded, feeling a pang in her heart. She knew Derik was right; they had to keep their professional relationship intact first and foremost. Anything else could wait for later on down the road if it was meant to be.

"That's true," she said, sighing a little sadly as her hopes plummeted back down to reality. "I agree, we should just be professionals. But I wanted you to know."

It was a bad idea to complicate things, and Morgan knew that. Still, part of her, deep inside, hoped this could be something more. It was ridiculous, though. Derik had told her about his divorce. He wasn't interested in love anymore, and maybe that would never change.

"It's not that I don't feel the same," Derik said. "I do. It's just a bad idea for both of us."

"You most of all?" Morgan asked, feeling bold.

Derik laughed. "Yeah. I told you about the divorce. I haven't exactly moved on. I know I need therapy, but ..."

Morgan nodded sympathetically. "I understand," she said. "I'm here for you if you ever need to talk about it. And believe me, if anyone needs therapy, it's me."

Derik smiled at her, his eyes softening. "Thanks, Cross. I appreciate that."

Morgan smiled back at him, feeling a sense of relief that they had talked about it. Even if they couldn't be anything more than just partners right now, at least they had been honest with each other. And that was the most important thing.

"What ended up happening to Sarah?" Morgan asked.

"She's grateful," Derik said. "I got to talk to her, but she wants to talk to you. We'll set up a visit when you're feeling up to it."

Morgan nodded, feeling grateful that Sarah was okay. At least she'd been able to save one person's life. Although there were four innocent women who had lost theirs, and Morgan wouldn't forget them.

But for now, she was just grateful to have Derik by her side. Maybe things weren't perfect, and they still had a long way to go. But for now, she was content just to be with Derik, and to know that they were in this together.

They sat in comfortable silence for a few more minutes before Derik stood up. "I should probably get going," he said. "But I'll check in on you tomorrow, okay?"

Morgan nodded. "Okay. Thanks again for everything, Derik."

"Anytime," he said with a smile before turning to leave.

Morgan watched him go with a twinge of sadness in her heart. She couldn't help the way she felt about him, but she knew she had to put those feelings aside and focus on their work. They had a job to do, and they couldn't afford to let anything get in the way of that. She hoped things wouldn't be off between them now that she'd confessed her feelings. And she hoped she could keep relying on him, especially if he was going to help her figure out who the hell framed her that night.

Suddenly, Skunk barked at the door. Morgan looked over just as there was a knock at the door.

"It's okay, boy," Morgan said, "just Derik. Maybe he forgot something."

She went over to the door, smiling as she opened it up. Skunk's barks grew louder, more anxious.

She expected to see Derik. But the face Morgan saw was like looking into the eyes of a ghost.

Darren La Roux.

An ex-con she'd helped put away, years ago.

But that wasn't all.

He held a gun up to Morgan, and she found herself staring down the barrel.

NOW AVAILABLE!

FOR LUST
(A Morgan Cross FBI Suspense Thriller—Book Three)

Victims of a new a serial killer found eerily propped up in movie theatres. A killer who will stop at nothing. An ex-con FBI agent with nothing left to lose….

"A masterpiece of thriller and mystery."
—Books and Movie Reviews, Roberto Mattos (re Once Gone)

FOR LUST is book #3 in a long-anticipated new series by #1 bestseller and USA Today bestselling author Blake Pierce, whose bestseller Once Gone (a free download) has received over 7,000 five star ratings and reviews.

Superstar FBI Agent Morgan Cross was at the height of her career when she was framed, wrongly imprisoned, and sent to do 10 hard years in prison. Finally exonerated and set free, Morgan emerges from jail as a changed person—hardened, ruthless, closed off to the world, and unsure how to start again. When the FBI comes knocking, desperately needing Morgan to return and hunt down a killer leaving bodies in movie theaters, Morgan is torn.

Morgan is not the same person, no longer willing to play by the rules, and will stop at nothing this time. In a non-stop thriller, it will be a deadly cat and mouse chase between a diabolical killer and an ex-con FBI agent who has nothing left to lose—with a new victim's fate riding on it all.

A page-turning and harrowing crime thriller featuring a brilliant and tortured FBI agent, the Morgan Cross series is a riveting mystery, packed with non-stop action, suspense, twists and turns, revelations, and driven by a breakneck pace that will keep you flipping pages late into the night. Fans of Rachel Caine, Teresa Driscoll and Robert Dugoni are sure to fall in love.

Future books in the series are also available!

"An edge of your seat thriller in a new series that keeps you turning pages! ...So many twists, turns and red herrings… I can't wait to see what happens next."
—Reader review (Her Last Wish)

"A strong, complex story about two FBI agents trying to stop a serial killer. If you want an author to capture your attention and have you guessing, yet trying to put the pieces together, Pierce is your author!"
—Reader review (Her Last Wish)

"A typical Blake Pierce twisting, turning, roller coaster ride suspense thriller. Will have you turning the pages to the last sentence of the last chapter!!!"
—Reader review (City of Prey)

"Right from the start we have an unusual protagonist that I haven't seen done in this genre before. The action is nonstop… A very atmospheric novel that will keep you turning pages well into the wee hours."
—Reader review (City of Prey)

"Everything that I look for in a book… a great plot, interesting characters, and grabs your interest right away. The book moves along at a breakneck pace and stays that way until the end. Now on go I to book two!"
—Reader review (Girl, Alone)

"Exciting, heart pounding, edge of your seat book… a must read for mystery and suspense readers!"
—Reader review (Girl, Alone)

Blake Pierce

Blake Pierce is the USA Today bestselling author of the RILEY PAGE mystery series, which includes seventeen books. Blake Pierce is also the author of the MACKENZIE WHITE mystery series, comprising fourteen books; of the AVERY BLACK mystery series, comprising six books; of the KERI LOCKE mystery series, comprising five books; of the MAKING OF RILEY PAIGE mystery series, comprising six books; of the KATE WISE mystery series, comprising seven books; of the CHLOE FINE psychological suspense mystery, comprising six books; of the JESSIE HUNT psychological suspense thriller series, comprising twenty-eight books; of the AU PAIR psychological suspense thriller series, comprising three books; of the ZOE PRIME mystery series, comprising six books; of the ADELE SHARP mystery series, comprising sixteen books, of the EUROPEAN VOYAGE cozy mystery series, comprising six books; of the LAURA FROST FBI suspense thriller, comprising eleven books; of the ELLA DARK FBI suspense thriller, comprising fourteen books (and counting); of the A YEAR IN EUROPE cozy mystery series, comprising nine books, of the AVA GOLD mystery series, comprising six books; of the RACHEL GIFT mystery series, comprising ten books (and counting); of the VALERIE LAW mystery series, comprising nine books (and counting); of the PAIGE KING mystery series, comprising eight books (and counting); of the MAY MOORE mystery series, comprising eleven books; of the CORA SHIELDS mystery series, comprising eight books (and counting); of the NICKY LYONS mystery series, comprising eight books (and counting), of the CAMI LARK mystery series, comprising eight books (and counting), of the AMBER YOUNG mystery series, comprising five books (and counting), of the DAISY FORTUNE mystery series, comprising five books (and counting), of the FIONA RED mystery series, comprising eight books (and counting), of the FAITH BOLD mystery series, comprising eight books (and counting), of the JULIETTE HART mystery series, comprising five books (and counting), of the MORGAN CROSS mystery series, comprising five books (and counting), and of the new FINN WRIGHT mystery series, comprising five books (and counting).

An avid reader and lifelong fan of the mystery and thriller genres, Blake loves to hear from you, so please feel free to visit www.blakepierceauthor.com to learn more and stay in touch.

BOOKS BY BLAKE PIERCE

FINN WRIGHT MYSTERY SERIES
WHEN YOU'RE MINE (Book #1)
WHEN YOU'RE SAFE (Book #2)
WHEN YOU'RE CLOSE (Book #3)
WHEN YOU'RE SLEEPING (Book #4)
WHEN YOU'RE SANE (Book #5)

MORGAN CROSS MYSTERY SERIES
FOR YOU (Book #1)
FOR RAGE (Book #2)
FOR LUST (Book #3)
FOR WRATH (Book #4)
FOREVER (Book #5)

JULIETTE HART MYSTERY SERIES
NOTHING TO FEAR (Book #1)
NOTHING THERE (Book #2)
NOTHING WATCHING (Book #3)
NOTHING HIDING (Book #4)
NOTHING LEFT (Book #5)

FAITH BOLD MYSTERY SERIES
SO LONG (Book #1)
SO COLD (Book #2)
SO SCARED (Book #3)
SO NORMAL (Book #4)
SO FAR GONE (Book #5)
SO LOST (Book #6)
SO ALONE (Book #7)
SO FORGOTTEN (Book #8)

FIONA RED MYSTERY SERIES
LET HER GO (Book #1)

LET HER BE (Book #2)
LET HER HOPE (Book #3)
LET HER WISH (Book #4)
LET HER LIVE (Book #5)
LET HER RUN (Book #6)
LET HER HIDE (Book #7)
LET HER BELIEVE (Book #8)

DAISY FORTUNE MYSTERY SERIES
NEED YOU (Book #1)
CLAIM YOU (Book #2)
CRAVE YOU (Book #3)
CHOOSE YOU (Book #4)
CHASE YOU (Book #5)

AMBER YOUNG MYSTERY SERIES
ABSENT PITY (Book #1)
ABSENT REMORSE (Book #2)
ABSENT FEELING (Book #3)
ABSENT MERCY (Book #4)
ABSENT REASON (Book #5)

CAMI LARK MYSTERY SERIES
JUST ME (Book #1)
JUST OUTSIDE (Book #2)
JUST RIGHT (Book #3)
JUST FORGET (Book #4)
JUST ONCE (Book #5)
JUST HIDE (Book #6)
JUST NOW (Book #7)
JUST HOPE (Book #8)

NICKY LYONS MYSTERY SERIES
ALL MINE (Book #1)
ALL HIS (Book #2)
ALL HE SEES (Book #3)
ALL ALONE (Book #4)
ALL FOR ONE (Book #5)
ALL HE TAKES (Book #6)

ALL FOR ME (Book #7)
ALL IN (Book #8)

CORA SHIELDS MYSTERY SERIES
UNDONE (Book #1)
UNWANTED (Book #2)
UNHINGED (Book #3)
UNSAID (Book #4)
UNGLUED (Book #5)
UNSTABLE (Book #6)
UNKNOWN (Book #7)
UNAWARE (Book #8)

MAY MOORE SUSPENSE THRILLER
NEVER RUN (Book #1)
NEVER TELL (Book #2)
NEVER LIVE (Book #3)
NEVER HIDE (Book #4)
NEVER FORGIVE (Book #5)
NEVER AGAIN (Book #6)
NEVER LOOK BACK (Book #7)
NEVER FORGET (Book #8)
NEVER LET GO (Book #9)
NEVER PRETEND (Book #10)
NEVER HESITATE (Book #11)

PAIGE KING MYSTERY SERIES
THE GIRL HE PINED (Book #1)
THE GIRL HE CHOSE (Book #2)
THE GIRL HE TOOK (Book #3)
THE GIRL HE WISHED (Book #4)
THE GIRL HE CROWNED (Book #5)
THE GIRL HE WATCHED (Book #6)
THE GIRL HE WANTED (Book #7)
THE GIRL HE CLAIMED (Book #8)

VALERIE LAW MYSTERY SERIES
NO MERCY (Book #1)
NO PITY (Book #2)

NO FEAR (Book #3)
NO SLEEP (Book #4)
NO QUARTER (Book #5)
NO CHANCE (Book #6)
NO REFUGE (Book #7)
NO GRACE (Book #8)
NO ESCAPE (Book #9)

RACHEL GIFT MYSTERY SERIES
HER LAST WISH (Book #1)
HER LAST CHANCE (Book #2)
HER LAST HOPE (Book #3)
HER LAST FEAR (Book #4)
HER LAST CHOICE (Book #5)
HER LAST BREATH (Book #6)
HER LAST MISTAKE (Book #7)
HER LAST DESIRE (Book #8)
HER LAST REGRET (Book #9)
HER LAST HOUR (Book #10)

AVA GOLD MYSTERY SERIES
CITY OF PREY (Book #1)
CITY OF FEAR (Book #2)
CITY OF BONES (Book #3)
CITY OF GHOSTS (Book #4)
CITY OF DEATH (Book #5)
CITY OF VICE (Book #6)

A YEAR IN EUROPE
A MURDER IN PARIS (Book #1)
DEATH IN FLORENCE (Book #2)
VENGEANCE IN VIENNA (Book #3)
A FATALITY IN SPAIN (Book #4)

ELLA DARK FBI SUSPENSE THRILLER
GIRL, ALONE (Book #1)
GIRL, TAKEN (Book #2)
GIRL, HUNTED (Book #3)
GIRL, SILENCED (Book #4)

GIRL, VANISHED (Book 5)
GIRL ERASED (Book #6)
GIRL, FORSAKEN (Book #7)
GIRL, TRAPPED (Book #8)
GIRL, EXPENDABLE (Book #9)
GIRL, ESCAPED (Book #10)
GIRL, HIS (Book #11)
GIRL, LURED (Book #12)
GIRL, MISSING (Book #13)
GIRL, UNKNOWN (Book #14)

LAURA FROST FBI SUSPENSE THRILLER
ALREADY GONE (Book #1)
ALREADY SEEN (Book #2)
ALREADY TRAPPED (Book #3)
ALREADY MISSING (Book #4)
ALREADY DEAD (Book #5)
ALREADY TAKEN (Book #6)
ALREADY CHOSEN (Book #7)
ALREADY LOST (Book #8)
ALREADY HIS (Book #9)
ALREADY LURED (Book #10)
ALREADY COLD (Book #11)

EUROPEAN VOYAGE COZY MYSTERY SERIES
MURDER (AND BAKLAVA) (Book #1)
DEATH (AND APPLE STRUDEL) (Book #2)
CRIME (AND LAGER) (Book #3)
MISFORTUNE (AND GOUDA) (Book #4)
CALAMITY (AND A DANISH) (Book #5)
MAYHEM (AND HERRING) (Book #6)

ADELE SHARP MYSTERY SERIES
LEFT TO DIE (Book #1)
LEFT TO RUN (Book #2)
LEFT TO HIDE (Book #3)
LEFT TO KILL (Book #4)
LEFT TO MURDER (Book #5)
LEFT TO ENVY (Book #6)

LEFT TO LAPSE (Book #7)
LEFT TO VANISH (Book #8)
LEFT TO HUNT (Book #9)
LEFT TO FEAR (Book #10)
LEFT TO PREY (Book #11)
LEFT TO LURE (Book #12)
LEFT TO CRAVE (Book #13)
LEFT TO LOATHE (Book #14)
LEFT TO HARM (Book #15)
LEFT TO RUIN (Book #16)

THE AU PAIR SERIES
ALMOST GONE (Book#1)
ALMOST LOST (Book #2)
ALMOST DEAD (Book #3)

ZOE PRIME MYSTERY SERIES
FACE OF DEATH (Book#1)
FACE OF MURDER (Book #2)
FACE OF FEAR (Book #3)
FACE OF MADNESS (Book #4)
FACE OF FURY (Book #5)
FACE OF DARKNESS (Book #6)

A JESSIE HUNT PSYCHOLOGICAL SUSPENSE SERIES
THE PERFECT WIFE (Book #1)
THE PERFECT BLOCK (Book #2)
THE PERFECT HOUSE (Book #3)
THE PERFECT SMILE (Book #4)
THE PERFECT LIE (Book #5)
THE PERFECT LOOK (Book #6)
THE PERFECT AFFAIR (Book #7)
THE PERFECT ALIBI (Book #8)
THE PERFECT NEIGHBOR (Book #9)
THE PERFECT DISGUISE (Book #10)
THE PERFECT SECRET (Book #11)
THE PERFECT FAÇADE (Book #12)
THE PERFECT IMPRESSION (Book #13)
THE PERFECT DECEIT (Book #14)

THE PERFECT MISTRESS (Book #15)
THE PERFECT IMAGE (Book #16)
THE PERFECT VEIL (Book #17)
THE PERFECT INDISCRETION (Book #18)
THE PERFECT RUMOR (Book #19)
THE PERFECT COUPLE (Book #20)
THE PERFECT MURDER (Book #21)
THE PERFECT HUSBAND (Book #22)
THE PERFECT SCANDAL (Book #23)
THE PERFECT MASK (Book #24)
THE PERFECT RUSE (Book #25)
THE PERFECT VENEER (Book #26)
THE PERFECT PEOPLE (Book #27)
THE PERFECT WITNESS (Book #28)

CHLOE FINE PSYCHOLOGICAL SUSPENSE SERIES
NEXT DOOR (Book #1)
A NEIGHBOR'S LIE (Book #2)
CUL DE SAC (Book #3)
SILENT NEIGHBOR (Book #4)
HOMECOMING (Book #5)
TINTED WINDOWS (Book #6)

KATE WISE MYSTERY SERIES
IF SHE KNEW (Book #1)
IF SHE SAW (Book #2)
IF SHE RAN (Book #3)
IF SHE HID (Book #4)
IF SHE FLED (Book #5)
IF SHE FEARED (Book #6)
IF SHE HEARD (Book #7)

THE MAKING OF RILEY PAIGE SERIES
WATCHING (Book #1)
WAITING (Book #2)
LURING (Book #3)
TAKING (Book #4)
STALKING (Book #5)
KILLING (Book #6)

RILEY PAIGE MYSTERY SERIES
ONCE GONE (Book #1)
ONCE TAKEN (Book #2)
ONCE CRAVED (Book #3)
ONCE LURED (Book #4)
ONCE HUNTED (Book #5)
ONCE PINED (Book #6)
ONCE FORSAKEN (Book #7)
ONCE COLD (Book #8)
ONCE STALKED (Book #9)
ONCE LOST (Book #10)
ONCE BURIED (Book #11)
ONCE BOUND (Book #12)
ONCE TRAPPED (Book #13)
ONCE DORMANT (Book #14)
ONCE SHUNNED (Book #15)
ONCE MISSED (Book #16)
ONCE CHOSEN (Book #17)

MACKENZIE WHITE MYSTERY SERIES
BEFORE HE KILLS (Book #1)
BEFORE HE SEES (Book #2)
BEFORE HE COVETS (Book #3)
BEFORE HE TAKES (Book #4)
BEFORE HE NEEDS (Book #5)
BEFORE HE FEELS (Book #6)
BEFORE HE SINS (Book #7)
BEFORE HE HUNTS (Book #8)
BEFORE HE PREYS (Book #9)
BEFORE HE LONGS (Book #10)
BEFORE HE LAPSES (Book #11)
BEFORE HE ENVIES (Book #12)
BEFORE HE STALKS (Book #13)
BEFORE HE HARMS (Book #14)

AVERY BLACK MYSTERY SERIES
CAUSE TO KILL (Book #1)
CAUSE TO RUN (Book #2)

CAUSE TO HIDE (Book #3)
CAUSE TO FEAR (Book #4)
CAUSE TO SAVE (Book #5)
CAUSE TO DREAD (Book #6)

KERI LOCKE MYSTERY SERIES
A TRACE OF DEATH (Book #1)
A TRACE OF MURDER (Book #2)
A TRACE OF VICE (Book #3)
A TRACE OF CRIME (Book #4)
A TRACE OF HOPE (Book #5)

Manufactured by Amazon.ca
Acheson, AB

12850036R00097